Mother Sawtooth's Nome
A novel of Alaskan history

James A. von der Heydt
Illustrations by the author

Oak Woods Media, Inc.

Copyright © 1990 by James A. von der Heydt
All rights reserved

Illustrations by the author

Except for appropriate use in critical reviews or works of scholarship, reproduction of any part of this book in any form requires written permission from the publisher.

Library of Congress Cataloging-in-Publication Data

von der Heydt, James A., 1919-
    Mother Sawtooth's Nome : a novel of Alaskan history / James A. von der Heydt : illustrations by the author.
        p.   cm.
    ISBN 0-88196-003-9 : $7.95
    1. Nome (Alaska)--History--Fiction. I. Title.
    PS3572.0424M6 1990
    813' .54--dc20   90-7323
                                                      CIP

ISBN 0-88196-003-9

Printed in the United States of America

Published by Oak Woods Media, Inc.
PO Box 527
Oshtemo, MI 49077
(616) 375-5621

This book lovingly is dedicated to my dear wife, Verna, who had the courage to say, "yes" and travel from Chicago to Nome as a bride, to share my life in one of the most fascinating places in the world.

This is a work of fiction and any resemblance between the characters herein and real persons is merely coincidental.

Foreword

In a city the size of Nome there are no strangers. So it is with surprise and delight that in my imagination I think I recognize, in this fictional account, people and events I have known. The author, aware that fiction is the ultimate truth, describes our city with hilarious hyperbole. Yet his own experience brings an honest respect that could only be an invitation to come and join us.

Nome, with its rampant gold rush history, its turmoil without legitimate leadership, and its continuing international fame is hardly the typical four-poster, one-red-light, midwestern town.

Some things about our city have changed in nearly a century, while others remain the same. The new Nome, unlike many boom towns that have become ghost towns, is built firmly upon the indelible permafrost foundation of the old.

As crazy as it sounds—as true as it has been, we are what we are—we are what we were.

—Leo Rasmussen, Mayor, City of Nome, 1977-1985

You can't get by with anything in Nome. In the summer it's light all the time, in winter you leave tracks.

—*Old sourdough saying*

Going Home

It was a returning and yet, in its way, a beginning, too. I was going back to Nome, back after an absence of several years. The lure of the quaint little town on the shore of Alaska's Bering Sea had stayed with me. Always I knew I would return, to live there, to find again the memories of my beloved Mother Sawtooth. Strange, recalling what an important part of my life she had been, I had difficulty picturing her now. I wanted to see Sawtooth House, to find Harvey, Eureka, Prybar and the others. I wanted to renew friendships with them all. And too, as the plane hummed its way toward Nome, I reflected upon my efforts to compile a cookbook of Mother Sawtooth's exceptional recipes. Surely, it was an endeavor worthy of her talents.

I recalled the first time I had flown to Nome, in the early forties. World War II was at its peak and Pan American Airways flew infrequently from Fairbanks in its tiny, twin-tailed silver Electras. I was working war construction, contracted to drive truck in the building of Marks Air Force Base. I remembered looking from the window to see the small speck of dark on the horizon grow with lessening distance to become Nome—a cluster of frame, shingle, and tarpaper-covered buildings crowding the beach. The plane flew low on its approach to the precarious runway, still under major construction. Houses, dirt streets, telephone poles with sagging wires, a garage here, filling station, store front, river, then lagoon, whizzed by in short profusion until the plane, low to the surface, reached earth with screeching wheels and pulling brakes.

A quick turnaround brought us to a small, wooden, one-room building, at that time the terminal for civilian aircraft. The nine or ten passengers aboard, a full load, gawked in awe at summertime Nome. Grass and bushes, a few scrubby willows in the gulleys nearby bent in the wind. Ground staff in warm parkas moved toward the plane. It was June, mid-June, but the wind spoke of the arctic. I noted unmelted drifts of snow in the shadows of buildings and in other places protected from the sun's penetration. It came to me a friend had said that if one lived in the arctic, one should expect arctic weather. Nome proved the point.

Now I was going back. I had written my story of those first Nome years, of Sawtooth House and dear Mother Sawtooth. It was the story of time gone forever, of the old Nome I then had known.

By chance, it was mid-June again. The plane touched down. I was home.

1

For those few persons who are not familiar with the Nome scene of the early forties, perhaps some words of explanation are necessary. Mother Sawtooth, of course, was a part of it all. To know Nome in those years was to know Mother, for Sawtooth House was a favorite gathering place for all who wanted pleasant rooming facilities, but most of all, for those who treasured gourmet dining. If one roomed at Mother's, one had the most prestigious Nome address on Third Avenue.

But another word or two about Nome before we begin that wonderful tongue-tingling trip through the recipes produced in Mother's kitchen. I hope you won't be impatient that we don't get right to the pan and skillet, but the background of these treasured recipes is important, too.

Nome, Alaska, that wonderful golden gold rush town, tipping the edge of the Bering Sea, awash in the sands of its famous beach. Streets of pure mud, the homes and buildings clapboard and unpainted. No water or sewage system. Oh, the romance of it all! The pure classic line of the fifty-five-gallon oil drum to be seen everywhere. Who can forget the Dream Theater, large and imposing, showing a film every Friday and Saturday night, the Bonanza Hotel, right on Front Street, awkward of line, covered with red brick siding, loose at the corners. And the Nome Bakery and Coffee House, its attractive metal-topped tables stained with food and drink of a bygone era, its wobbly wooden chairs and its menu, unchanged since 1913. Such was the Nome of the early forties.

But there was more: The saloons of Nome, rickity-ticky, smelling of stale tobacco and beer, sticky floors, the home of the juke box and the wailing cowboy song. Such names as the Glue Pot, the Traders, the Nugget, and the Golden Egg are etched on the memory of every Nomeite. The owner and chief bartender of the Glue Pot, certainly Nome's most popular retreat, was Paddy O'Brien. Paddy was a tall man, well put together, with a gleaming Irish eye, whose most prized accouterment was his immense walrus mustache. Paddy knew the world.

"A town's no good," he would say, "unless there's a saloon for every church."

Nome qualified.

By design, Paddy's bartending talents were basic. He served beer, several different whiskies, and a violent red wine for the "non-drinkers," which he poured from a large unlabeled jug kept under the bar. A newcomer once ordered scotch and soda. Paddy blanched, rested both hands on the bar, leaned close to the unfortunate neophite and shouted, "Look, bud, none of those fancy mixed drinks in here!" Ah, Nome, what loving memories.

The founders of the city in the early 1900s were men of vision who could see clearly. They sensed that Nome was to go on to greatness and rightly so. Their foresight is evident in the naming of the streets. North and south the streets were lettered, and east and west the streets were numbered. No problem here with some future city clerk wasting time and effort to envision novel street names! The founders' wisdom has been borne out. The lettered streets extend to "D" and the numbered to "5". Plenty of room for unrestricted expansion. The exception, of course, was the main thoroughfare, Front Street, so named because it parallels the beach and thus fronts the town. It has been said that the early Nome gold stampeders brought the name with them from Dawson City, but no proof of this accusation of Klondike plagiarism is available.

Thinking back now about Mother Sawtooth and Nome, I remember the magnificent home she maintained on Third Avenue. Large, with a second story over the first, "Sawtooth House" was an imposing structure. Because of the permafrost and the fact that Harvey had never gotten around to jacking up and leveling the west side, the place tilted to the west rather noticeably. But this concerned no one unless Mother was going to serve one of her famous and well known soups in her shallow soup plates.

Inside, Sawtooth House was well appointed with furniture of modern design from the Victorian era. Crisp, starched damask drapes hung at the windows of the living room, giving the place an air of regal elegance. The floors were carpeted with throw rugs imported from Seattle. The dining room, of course the most important room in Mother Sawtooth's house, contained a boxwood edelshelf upon which always sat an inviting bowl of wax oranges. And the table, that famous table, accompanied by eight reedback chairs, was covered with dark green ("legume colored," Mother always called it) oil cloth, elegantly cut at each end. A beautiful single candle made of real candle wax was the centerpiece. The inspiration of this table as it held Mother's famous culinary achievements and cooking was instantly apparent to the beholder.

Now to Mother's kitchen, that wondrous room from which came forth and emitted those heavenly aromas and odors of gastronomic works of art. Surprisingly, the kitchen was a rather small room not too large. Her oil range, converted from coal to oil when the latter became plentiful, sat against the far wall, with a white kitchen table, light in color, opposite. The floor was covered with gay gray linoleum which had buckled to some extent because of the westward tilt of the room. But no matter to Mother Sawtooth! From that room forever poured an unending variety of delectables. Soups, roullinaides, petty-nois, grenillas of beef, pork or sanderling, cakes, pastries de fromage or cheese, and racks of barquet or brillo. All emerged from that kitchen to the applause and hand clapping of our cheery faces. Oh, Mother Sawtooth, how did you ever accomplish and do such wondrous things?

And now a word about Mother Sawtooth herself, for I have told little about her. I know you are anxious. Roly-poly and plump, short and of limited stature, she had a pleasant face with pleasant enough facial features and naturally gray and frizzy hair that was usually pulled together in back rather unsuccessfully into a bun or roll. Her active hands were ever busy about the place, a pinch of grenoble here, a touch of lauderlous there, just enough always, never too much and not too little. Culinarily speaking, she had no equal, nor could anyone match her abilities in the kitchen.

Harvey was Mother's boyfriend and male companion. I presume this is not getting too personal, but of all her admirers Harvey appeared to be the most successful. He had come mysteriously from the gold creeks outlying Nome, tall, noble, strong, and without an ambitious bone in his body. He needed someone to lean upon and to brace him, and he fell for Mother at first glance. Somehow, too, Mother needed him, for she was lonely in her great talent, and the house needed leveling. Harvey moved in the second night, right after dinner, and it was said by Nome's ready gossips that he was her paramour. Gracious! This is bordering on gossip, to which I strongly object, so perhaps only a little more will bring the situation into clean focus and render it understandable. To be candid and truthful, Harvey and Mother shared the same bedroom. This arrangement generally was frowned upon by most Nomeites. But who is to judge, who is to say, "Wrong, wrong, wrong!" Shirley, not I.

Shirley was my girl in those days. We had a candid and open relationship observable to all, which we kept as secret as possible. At Mother Sawtooth's there was little criticism because few if any of her boarders lived in solitude or alone.

I had liked Shirley all along. Our relationship nurtured and blossomed like an opening door. She had been a dance hall girl at the Glue Pot, where she affectionately was known as "Piano Legs," a Nomenclature she did not especially enjoy. I met her one evening when new to Mother's establishment, and when Shirley learned of my residence, she indeed was impressed. As is well known, the life of a dance hall girl in Nome, Alaska in those years was no easy caper. Dresses, hose and shoes had to be kept presentable and frankly, Shirley was getting a bit shabby. She was ready for a change.

She had come on the stage to the happy shouts of the customers of the Glue Pot, "Not old Piano Legs again!" I watched her careful performance and observed immediately that, although talent of the dance had shorted her, she possessed other obvious attributes and attractions.

Shirley was mine. But I have been distracted. I should return to the description of Mother's house, as a true understanding of this showplace is necessary to grasp the import of the gastronomic masterpieces to be described on the coming pages.

The upstairs bedrooms were reached by a narrow staircase that turned at right angles near the top. Mother's and Harvey's room, of course, was the largest and faced the front of the house. Mother recently had moved the bed from the west to the east wall of the room, because, as she noted, she found it uncomfortable to sleep with her head lower than her feet. Harvey complained of the change, but to no avail. He continued to come home after an evening with Paddy, only to fall on the non-existent bed at the west side of the room. We all could hear this nightly thump, and knew at last we could lapse into undisturbed slumber. Mother's room also contained a beautiful piece of furniture—a large argentian burokoff with five drawers—on top of which she kept one of her most prized possessions, a brush and mirror set of genuine plastic, given by Millwood the first birthday he had stayed with her.

Millwood had taken Harvey's place in the household only two days after Harvey left for his summer endeavor in the Kougarok gold fields north of Nome. Harvey and Otis Updown had maintained some placer claims on Dahl Creek for many years, but although adjoining claims worked by others had produced remarkable results, neither Harvey nor Otis could seem to get the mining season started before freezeup. Their grubstakes as well as the summer gone, they returned to Nome with detailed plans for the next year's successful operation.

At any rate, a bit more about Millwood before we get to Mother Sawtooth's unequaled kitchen creations. Millwood was a powdered milk salesman, whom the autumn before, had over-partaken of Paddy's wares and thus missed the last boat to Seattle. His employer had chafed at his failure to return from Nome, and had terminated his services without curds or whey. Millwood was stranded, and spent a miserable winter sharing a minimal existance with a friend who lived in a one-room log cabin on a beach west of town, and who could cook no better than he could.

Millwood, of course, had heard of Mother Sawtooth and her famous kitchen. When he learned that Harvey had departed for the creek, he moved with speed and alacrity of foot to take his place in Mother's bed, but more importantly, at Mother's table. He was thin as a needle.

We never knew whether Millwood was Millwood's first or last name. He simply introduced himself as Millwood and once when someone asked, he responded, "My name is Millwood." For this reason we all called him Millwood.

I suppose your pans and spoons are restless to get started down the path to one of Mother's famous old Nome recipes. Patience! It is important first to understand the background from whence these treasures came.

2

Eureka Tumok was a spritely Eskimo girl who helped Mother in the kitchen. She had the native's stocky build, round face and dark eyes and, like most, she was both friendly and shy. For a long time we thought Eureka was clairvoyant. Without apparent forethought, Eureka would volunteer news of happenings to come in the Nome world. Somehow she seemed to read the future. Strangely, these prognostications proved to be accurate when later we heard the radio news or read the latest edition of the Nome *Nugget*.

"The mail plane is weathered in at Moses Point," Eureka announced one evening while serving dinner. Millwood, well into his third helping of Mother's delicious crepes de renard in magrat sauce, took hold of Eureka's apron and held her immobile.

"Now just how do you know that?" Millwood asked a bit guardedly, for he knew her reputation for accuracy.

Eureka grinned and added. "The pilot's name is Glen Johnson and he's going to stay the night at Moses Point. He'll try again tomorrow."

Millwood, more interested in his crepes de renard than in the mail plane, released his hold and Eureka quickly disappeared into the kitchen. We were astonished when, a few minutes later, Elijah took his place at the dinner table, late as usual for he had to clean the honey bucket wagon before leaving work, and stated, "I heard, when I was at the airfield, that the mail plane is stuck at Moses Point. Johnson says the weather is so bad he won't even try to make Nome until tomorrow." There it was again. Somehow Eureka knew. A hard silence followed. Shirley dropped her fork which clattered onto her plate. Mother's eyes widened. I cleared my throat.

"Well, Jesus Christ!" exclaimed Millwood.

Eureka came into the room to serve coffee brichard. Eureka just smiled.

It was damnably annoying to have that girl doing that sort of thing all the time. Somehow we felt mysteriously inferior when she offered these pronouncements, which almost invariably proved to be accurate to the last detail.

Eureka had come to Nome a few weeks earlier from

the village of Shakaluk. She never had ventured from her own village before, but when her teeth began to bother her seriously, the Native Service arranged to bring her to Nome to see the dentist. In the opinion of Doc Slater, the local dentist, who had seen her immediately, she had been "brushing her teeth with her elbow." Thirteen fillings later, Eureka was pronounced dentally rescued but, when it came time to go home, she would not go. The bright lights of Nome had succeeded in dazzling her and she announced to a bewildered Native Service employee that she never wanted to see Shakaluk again.

Miss Pimworth, the Native Service employee, was panic stricken. What if Washington should learn of this, of her failure to convince this Eskimo girl that she must go home? After three sleepless nights a harrowed and hollow-eyed Miss Pimworth found an answer. Not *the* answer, but *an* answer better than total failure, as might otherwise be reflected in her superior's report to the Washington office. She would find Eureka a job. The girl would be productive and Miss Pimworth could put that in her own report. And so, to Mother's kitchen Eureka came, happily smiling, for at least Mother's kitchen was not Shakaluk.

As time went on, the situation with Eureka only got worse. Each evening she would relate to us the news to come. At last we raised courage enough to confront her concerning her annoying, but always accurate, statements. One evening, after a wonderful meal of colonaide of cock capon in sauce bernoose, Elijah asked Eureka the question.

"For God's sake, Eureka," he said, "you're about to drive us all to the looney bin. How do you know all these things?"

Eureka hesitated, and with the air of one expecting not to be believed, she said, "I hear the radio in my new teeth. The sounds come through my fillings."

A long silence followed. We all sat astounded, speechless. Millwood shifted in his chair and his inner bowel growled loud enough for all to hear. Eureka just smiled and began to clear away the plates.

3

Elijah Meek was a black man, for many years the only one in Nome. In the early forties he was called a negro, or colored, but those descriptions have given way to the modern terminology. Elijah was short and stocky, but extremely well muscled. He had been a professional boxer of sorts and roamed the lower forty-eight states for several years, picking up a paying fight here and there wherever he could find one.

Suddenly one day it occured to Elijah that he seldom had won a fight and aside from that, his nose was noticeably bent toward the left side of his face and he had a mild cauliflower ear. Sometimes, too, lately, after a particularly severe drubbing, he had trouble holding his feet or remembering his name. In a moment of clear thought, Elijah decided to quit the ring after his next fight. This decision was fortified when his opponent's manager, obviously not cognizant of his past fighting record, secretly offered him two hundred dollars to throw the fight. Elijah readily agreed, for two hundred dollars was more than he had ever earned from one fight and he was determined to keep his resolve to quit the fighting game.

The fight was over in the third round when Elijah, having put up weak resistance, found himself, as usual, on his back with a referee counting over him and a triumphant opponent dancing about the ring, hands held high.

Elijah took his two hundred dollars plus the twenty-five dollars paid by the promoters, and passed the next week nursing a bleeding nose and a particularly sensitive knob on the back of his head. His injuries passive, if not completely cured, he began to think of his future, since he no longer would be in the ring. He was thirty-one years old and he knew his nose and ear would never be other than bent and cauliflowered respectively. He had grand visions, but obviously Hollywood was out, even though he had a cousin who was doing well in the movies playing obedient butlers and houseboys.

His last fight had been in an old warehouse in Portland, Oregon, so for reasons unknown when later he thought on it, Elijah hitchhiked to Seattle to search for a job. He rode along the highway with an old apple farmer, the latter's battered pickup truck bouncing over the potholes and cracks in the road. He watched the lush green of the countryside move by, for the first time noticing the beautiful deep green spruce and pine. These scenes were new to Elijah's eyes as he had been raised on a desolate and dry plot of land in the most arid part of Texas, and rarely before in his travels had he taken the time to observe his surroundings with care.

The first day in Seattle, in a waterfront bar, Elijah was queried concerning his draft status by a determined, middle-aged lady who apparently was making the rounds for that purpose. Now the war was very much on, but Elijah had been a wanderer for years and he had never found time to register for military service. The lady's questioning made him nervous, for she wrote down everything and firmly instructed him to report forthwith to the Selective Service office on Union Street in downtown Seattle. Elijah knew he had to move on, and fast. He watched the lady leave the bar and turn to the south. Elijah left the bar and turned to the north. And north it was to be.

In the bar next door he met a man who was looking for an assistant oiler for a ship out of Seattle for Nome. Elijah had no idea what an assistant oiler did, or an oiler for that matter, but he quickly professed his experience and expertise and signed on. The thought of the Selective Service office on Union Street made him tense. The *S. S. Golden North* sailed at midnight with Elijah in the pounding engine room, an unfamiliar long-necked oil can in his hand. Most of the voyage passed with Elijah retching into the waste barrel, as he never had been to sea before and both the Gulf of Alaska and the Bering Sea were foaming and gray. Mercifully, 12 days later the *Golden North* anchored in the roadstead off Nome in relatively calm seas. Elijah, his eyes bloodshot and his stomach completely inverted, jumped the first barge to shore. He had no idea how he would get back to Seattle, but it was not to be on the *Golden North* or on any other sea-going vessel.

He walked down Nome's boardwalk on Front Street, sensing the nip of winter in the air, for it was mid-September. His path took him past the Arctic Trading Post, the Yukon Hardware, then the Nome Bakery. From the latter came the pleasant aroma of yeast and newly baked bread. Elijah quickly went on, as the odor of any food reminded him all too accurately of the fast-rolling sea and his equally fast-rolling stomach. Although in no sense prepared to eat, he realized that already his agonized digestive system seemed to be settling.

"Well," he said to himself almost audibly, "Nome, I'm here and I ain't going back. What's next?"

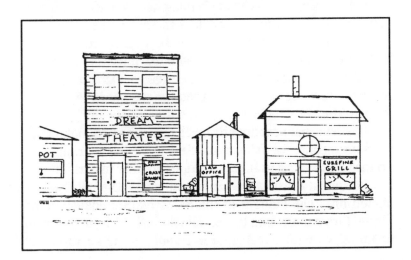

4

Next for Elijah was Cletus Strong. Cletus owned and operated the sanitary service or, more colloquially, the honey bucket wagon. Earlier, I have mentioned that Nome in those days had no water and sewer system. As it had been from the early gold rush days, and I hope not to be too indelicate since soon we are going to get to Mother Sawtooth's fabulous recipes, human waste was collected on a regular basis from each home or business establishment. Each had a so-called honey bucket tucked away under a normal toilet seat, available to the outside through a small hinged door. The bucket was removed, emptied into one of several fifty-five-gallon drums on the honey wagon, and returned to its slot.

It was rare that a newcomer to Nome was not stranded in an embarrassing and compromising position as the honey bucket was jerked unceremoniously from under him before he had completed nature's call. This is how Elijah met Cletus Strong.

Unfamiliar with Nome, Elijah had taken rather barren accommodations at the Mukluk Inn, one of the town's lesser rooming houses. After several days of light eating, finally his system began functioning again. His first need to relieve himself called him to one of the Mukluk Inn's cubicles. He was frustrated in traditional mid-passage when the small door suddenly flew open and with shattering, screeching clatter, the waiting receptacle was jerked from beneath his now-anxious bottom. Involuntarily, Elijah jumped from the seat, cracking his head on the closed door before him. Furious, and cursing audibly, he half gathered his trousers about him and charged outside. He met Cletus coming back, happily swinging the now empty bucket and merrily whistling a jaunty tune. Elijah's urge immediately was transferred to the need to clip this man with a boxer's good left hook, but to do so would have forced him to drop his trousers.

Cletus Strong saw him coming, sensed his predicament, laughed, pulled a grubby glove from his hand and extended it toward Elijah. Cletus was very tall, at least six feet four or five inches, with an irrepressible grin, white teeth, and a tattered cowboy hat pushed to the back of his head. Elijah's anger wilted. He firmly gripped his loosened pants with his left hand and took Cletus in a firm handshake.

They became lifelong friends, but Cletus never would allow Elijah to forget the circumstances of their meeting.

5

But I have wandered from Mother Sawtooth and I must get back to her. There is so much to tell about Nome, and the excitement of Sawtooth House, that I am tempted beyond the purpose of this book. After all, it is Mother's unique recipes that interest us, as these must be preserved for posterity, or for anyone else who has an interest in the art of the kitchen.

As time went by, and each evening we had gathered about the dinner table at Sawtooth House, the door to the kitchen would swing wide and Mother would enter with steaming platter or hot canbarr, followed, of course, by Eureka who carried the condiments, salads, and blanchards.

Thinking back now, who can forget Mother's champon of mitkin with salmon berries and gensing, her renault of goose and lumpkin smothered in auberge sauce, the marvelous saturnal of revolving crane with kesko and ramulet relish. Oh, to taste again that wonderful sweet pate of reeble onions covered with barbillo cream! How my gums water for a simple serving of filderlaud en morgols de tattons, served piping hot from the oven.

I strongly felt these priceless combinations of meats, pourris, potages, soups, scrimshaws and many others must be preserved on paper for others to savor. It was with this in mind that I timidly approached Mother one day with the suggestion that she should write down her magnificent combinations into usable recipes. She nodded as if in agreement, but her talents and sensitivities were so great that I knew I must proceed slowly. No pushing, I sensed, or all would be lost.

I decided to bide my time. At this point, it had been my plan to go directly to some of Mother Sawtooth's treasured and appetite-tempting creations but, since it will take time to compile these in a manner satisfactory to the reader, I first will begin the unusual story of Clover Blue Conzarro.

6

I know it is true because I observed it myself. The ladies of Nome's teacup society did not include Clover Blue Conzarro in the prominent social events of the community. It was not considered the proper thing to do.

Clover Blue had come to Nome following a blizzard of critical publicity in the newspapers of the nation, particularly those of the San Francisco area. Because of her intriguing name, unusual Alaskan background, and her once-prestigious position in the fascinating affairs of San Francisco's waterfront underworld, she had become a favorite public figure for wide press attention. Her unexpected appearance in Nome had set tongues in motion, as the local gossips were delighted to change from the rather mundane city happenings to so startling a new development. Speculation as to the reasons for the arrival of Clover Blue were rife in the community.

As weeks passed following her return, Clover Blue had found a small house on the edge of the little town, away from prattling neighbors and prying eyes. But her purposeful aloofness from the rest of the town's citizens had led to her exclusion from a majority of the city's events. For the most part, remembering all too keenly her unfortunate San Francisco experiences, Clover Blue welcomed this quiet isolation.

A notable exception was her close friendship with dear Mother Sawtooth. Mother's always keen and observant mind had found values in Clover Blue that others earnestly had overlooked. For this reason, on frequent occasions she had been invited by Mother Sawtooth to join us around her famous gastronomic table at Sawtooth House. It is, of course, Mother's renowned table and her fabulous recipes that are to win our full attention. These wonderful, tooth-watering endeavors will be revealed in due time.

One evening, Clover Blue had been included at Mother's for a delicious dinner of her widely acclaimed felicia of monsurrat beluga cheeks with trois pois. When the meal was finished, and Clover Blue had departed, we asked Mother why she liked Clover Blue and included her so often when there was so much gossip in the community about her. Mother, in her usual astute way, pondered the question for a moment. Then she spoke, as we all listened to her answer in the quiet of the room.

"What's goose to the gander is grease to the grinder," she said.

Of course, we should have known. The typical original, well thought-out and meaningful answer. How did she do it? We were impressed. Yes, those days with Mother Sawtooth indeed were unique and memorable.

But before going on to the pan, manton and darrinpot of Mother's truly remarkable kitchen, I should tell you more of the story of Clover Blue Conzarro. Surely it is not fair to do otherwise.

We all knew Clover Blue, were aware of her background and of the problems that led to her return to Nome. The thrice weekly published *Nome Nugget* had kept the citizens of the town well- informed.

Clover Blue had arrived "back home" unannounced on the *North Star's* final voyage of the season. According to a pursuing press, Clover Blue had disappeared from the San Francisco area leaving no trace of her whereabouts and no hint of her future plans. She was the widow of Tony "Hot Sheets" Conzarro, noted boss of San Francisco's underworld.

Tony had become "Hot Sheets" to the world following a press interview with Madelaine Good, his former live-in girlfriend. Madelaine had wandered to Los Angeles and San Francisco from Brooklyn as a twenty-year-old, whose body belonged on every cinema screen of the nation, but whose mind was not capable of remembering a line of dialogue long enough to get a movie camera in operation.

A reporter from the *Daily Free Press* had offered Madelaine fifty dollars for an interview in which she was to tell all she knew about San Francisco rackets boss, Tony Conzarro. The result was mostly unprintable, but the statement that made the headlines and forever thereafter tagged Tony with his nickname, was Madelaine's passing observation that when one lived with Tony Conzarro, there always were hot sheets on the bed. It was by far the cleverest remark Madelaine had conjured up in her twenty-one years of life, and Tony never lived it down. In truth, at first the comment had annoyed him, but later he grew to rather enjoy its implications.

Clover Blue's relationship with Tony had brought her, at first, everything she could have hoped for in life and, finally, to a dismal end—Tony dead, his blood running across the sidewalk of a bleak and dirty Chinatown street. But she loved Tony dearly, and he fully had returned her affection. When he died he was the victim of an underworld plot to get rid of him, for he had become far too powerful and ruthless to remain alive. Clover Blue quickly had fled San Francisco with a few personal belongings, a small amount of cash, and the one thing she treasured most, a beautiful diamond ring Tony had given her as a wedding present. This she soon was forced to sell to a pawnbroker in Seattle for the cash she needed to support herself and escape to Nome where a hounding press was unlikely to follow her.

Now, in 1943, Clover Blue was thirty-five years of age, the snow of her native Alaska first touching the dark hair of her temples. She was tall for her half-Eskimo heritage, and she had learned early in life, as a waif growing up in Nome's river sandspit, that extra strength was expected of her and that loneliness would be hers to face and hers to overcome.

Even as a child, Clover Blue had sensed that she was attractive to men and, as she grew into her teen years, she learned to put this characteristic to good use. Actually, she was not startlingly beautiful in the sense of her good friend to be, Carlotta Sands, but there was something lovely and exotic about her that turned men's heads and brought her unexpected attention.

Clover Blue was the daughter of a bright-haired Irishman named Johnny McLauren and a full-blooded Eskimo, Edna Mayoktuk. Johnny had come to Nome for adventure as the agent of the Arctic Steamship Co. On a whim, he had married Edna, impregnated her with child, and promptly abandoned her when transferred back to Seattle.

For all her limited background and lack of formal education, Edna Mayoktuk was a woman of remarkable insight into the white man's world of Nome in which she lived—a characteristic not at all typical of Eskimo women of her time and generation. She spoke English well, could write her name, and judged the limitations which set her place in life with uncanny ability. Her marriage to a white man and its forseeable failure she accepted with stoic calm.

The child of the union, named Clover Blue, was born in a lean-to shack late one March evening, a blizzard raging outside the loosely-fitting door. No one knew the immediacy of Edna's labor, and so she had given birth to her little girl alone, as her own mother had given life to her, squatting low over the soft fur of reindeer hides, letting the infant slip unaided into a hostile, cold, and darkened world.

The child's eyes were blue, like her father's, but when she was only a few days old the color darkened and reminded Edna of the lovely violet-blue of the wild clover covering the rolling summer hills of the Alaskan tundra. At first, her mother wanted to name the baby Ellen, but the color of the infant's eyes was too compelling to overlook. The child had to be named Clover Blue and so she became. The unusual name was to mark the little girl throughout an eventful and unpredictable life.

When Clover Blue was seven years old, Edna, who never had been really content in Nome, decided to return to her own native village and to take the child with her. Clover Blue was too young to understand all the implications of this plan, but she knew in her young heart that she did not want to go. She early had learned that as a half-breed she was not white to the whites nor was she Eskimo to the natives. Neither race was willing to accept her as its own. Since she had lived her early years with her mother, who was full Eskimo, she naturally related to that race. She attended the Native School, operated by the federal government for native children. The Territorial School was reserved for whites.

It was a forceful and devoted teacher at the Native School who came forward to talk to Edna and convince her that Clover Blue should remain in Nome, at least to complete the eighth grade, the highest offered at the Native School. Miss Esther London fortunately had taught Clover Blue in the first and second grades. She found wonder in the bright and enthusiastic child with the creamy complexion, shiny auburn hair, and remarkable violet eyes. Miss London recognized a rare intelligence and an even more rare desire to learn. She convinced Edna to let Clover Blue remain in Nome, to live with Edna's brother and his family. To this plan Edna reluctantly agreed. To part with her daughter hurt Edna deeply, but she recognized, in an unspoken way she, herself, did not understand, that Clover Blue was not at all "native" as was her own heritage.

Thus, Clover Blue stayed on in Nome, living with her Uncle Walter, his wife and two sons. With tears restrained, Edna left the child standing on the beach at Nome, hand-in-hand with Miss London, as she boarded the coastal tug *Glacier Trader* for the three-day trip west, then around Cape Prince of Wales to the north, to her own village. Clover Blue had promised to write to her mother, which she did, but Edna's writing ability was so severely limited that she could not reply.

Uncle Walter and his family were agreeable to Clover Blue's presence, but the girl sensed profound differences between herself and the family members. She loved them as best she could for their kindness to her, but she knew she must leave their home as soon as possible to make her own way.

Unknown either to Edna or to Clover Blue, Esther London, that good and remarkable woman, delivered to Uncle Walter ten dollars each month from her own meager salary to aid in the support of Clover Blue. Miss London found, in teaching native children, a personal challenge many of her fellow teachers seldom realized. She inspired Clover Blue to discover, in the many books she brought her to read, a world wholly unknown—one that the child in the not too distant future determined to see and experience herself.

Following completion of the eighth grade, Clover Blue continued to read extensively from works of her own choosing and those recommended by Miss London. She taught herself some basics of high school algebra, history, and English composition, but reading alone could not satisfy her insatiable curiosity about the wondrous world outside Nome.

For several years, until she was 17, Clover Blue worked as a stock inventory clerk for O. O. Osterman, owner of the Nome Storage and Lighterage Co. Then suddenly, without detailed planning, she one day told "Old Triple O," as he was called by most of the community, that she was leaving

Nome on the *Victoria,* then anchored in the roadstead, soon to sail for Seattle. For unexplained reasons, San Francisco had become the idealized city of her dreams and she determined to travel there from Seattle as soon as possible.

Two years earlier, her beloved Miss London had retired and left Nome for her original home near Boston. Thus, with both her mother and Miss London gone, Clover Blue had little to keep her in Nome.

It was a foggy August morning that brought her to say goodbyes to Old Triple O and other friends and board the barge pulled onto the beach for transfer of passengers to the *Victoria.* In spite of her youth, Clover Blue was by then in all ways, a mature young woman.

She stood on the deck and watched the wake of the *Victoria* churn the Bering Sea into white, salty froth as the ship's engines moved into action. The vessel gained speed and she saw the little town of her birth and girlhood recede into the distance, finally to disappear in a flurry of mist, white gulls, and rolling sea. She watched for a long time, even after no trace of the land was visible, then turned away to an unknown new life in an unknown new world.

7

In the early days of the Nome gold bonanza, several hundred horses were brought by ship from the West Coast to the booming gold rush town. Billy Moore, the great teamster of early Nome, owned by far the largest stable, located at the east end of town and housing sixty or seventy animals. Billy's teams, sometimes twelve to twenty in harness, were needed to move heavy mining equipment from the beach, where it had been off-loaded from barges, to the mining camps, which sometimes were seventy-five to one hundred miles inland. Thousands of men and their supplies had poured ashore from the ships that came from Seattle and San

Francisco, and it has been estimated that Nome's population between 1901 and 1909 exceeded twenty-five thousand.

By the early forties the automobile and the motor truck had replaced the horses. Gravel roads of sorts had been built by the Alaska Road Commission to the most important mining areas, and so the horses' ability to travel cross-country without benefit of roads was no longer needed. The narrow gauge Kougarok Railroad had been constructed in the early years and this too provided transportation to important mining districts. Thus, the horse and the service it provided had become obsolete.

Billy Moore had been laid to rest at least fifteen years earlier in the cemetery at Belmont Point, his extensive stables torn down for the lumber and his beautiful dray horses sold locally or shipped back to the States.

When spring breakup arrived in 1943, only one horse remained in Nome, an old swayback roan named Prince. No one knew Prince's age or from where he had come. Prince pulled the honey bucket wagon and long years of practice had taught him each day's path. Without direction from Cletus, he knew by rote the different routes about town. In traditional manner, Cletus had provided Prince with an old, broad-brimmed straw hat, two large holes cut for his ears to poke through. Cletus, Prince, and his wagon were familiar to all. Prince knew the sounds, when to stop, when to go on, where to turn. Cletus loved old Prince dearly, for in Nome's coldest winter weather he never froze up and rarely became stuck in the heavy drifts of snow.

When Elijah came to work for Cletus, Prince had to become accustomed to him. Their first months together were not happy ones, for Prince was comfortable only with Cletus and was skittish around others. Finally however, after several months, Prince came to accept Elijah and even to take a carrot or sugar lump from his hand.

But age had come to Prince, year by year, and as time passed, both Cletus and Elijah noted the increasing difficulty the old fellow had in completing his daily rounds. Cletus, in hope of assistance, had sent for a mail order veterinarian book and rummaged it carefully for any suggested medication that might help Prince. There appeared to be none. In summary, the book made clear that when an animal had reached old age and was in failing health, no useful treatment was available.

Thus it was a difficult decision for both men, when it became obvious that Prince no longer was able to handle the daily rounds. Cletus and Elijah went to the stable together, rubbed the old horse's ears and fed him carrots and lumps of sugar. Prince's weakened legs barely could support his weight and somehow they thought he knew. He was to be replaced, as had been all his early day companions, by a truck.

8

It was about mid-summer when Prybar Plunkett came to live at Mother's. Oh, Prybar was not his true name, but a nickname he had picked up while working on one of the gold dredges north of town. Prybar's real name was Austin, but no one had called him that for years. He never really could decide whether he liked being called Prybar instead of Austin, but the nickname had stuck so hard it proved impossible to dislodge it.

Prybar took Elijah's place at table and bed when the latter got married, and moved to a home of his own, up on Fourth Avenue near the big mining company building. For several months, Elijah had been smitten of Darlene, a comely young Eskimo maiden who waited tables at the Surefine Grill. At first Darlene would have nothing to do with Elijah, but as time went by and he left larger and larger tips she began to notice him and agreed at last to become Mrs. Elijah Meek.

The wedding took place at the Federated United Native Church on the coldest night of the year. It was well over thirty degrees below zero, and Pastor Dade could not seem to keep the church's small, oil space heater in operation. So we all sat stiffly, clad in coats, boots and parkas, while the pastor labored through what proved to be an overly long ceremony. To make matters worse, Pastor Dade suffered from a tendency to stammer, and this unfortunate affliction was encouraged by the chilling temperature.

Darlene stood, shaking to the bone in her filmy white dress, while beside her stood good Elijah, too much in love to notice the cold. The pastor's G-G-G-Gods and p-p-p-prayers mercifully came to an end with a final b-b-b-blessing and we all repaired through a howling blizzard and climbed over snow drifts as high as the peaks of the houses to Mother Sawtooth's for a splendid wedding supper.

When all the guests had arrived and boots, mukluks and parkas were left in the entry cache, the folding doors to the dining room were opened. Candlelight cast softened shadows about the room and all were astonished at the beauty of the handmade and decorated lantolagels hanging everywhere. It was a notable and memorable sight.

Who can forget that table! It was laden from end to end with delectables only Mother Sawtooth could envision and create. A three-tiered wedding cake was placed on a pedestal in the center, resplendent in frosting de telebaum and sequins. Each dish around the table contained some delicious sweetmeat, epinard, peppermince, or candied comesquat. The coffee urn was draped in colored crepe paper streamers, beautifully done by Eureka. Champagne corks popped, for Mother wanted this to be an unforgettable evening.

It was, except for poor Elijah, whose stomach never really had been the same since his unfortunate voyage aboard the *Golden North*. Sadly, in his excitement, poor Elijah had overeaten, particularly of the comesquats, and the unhappy result was that he spent a major portion of his wedding night resting atop an all too familiar honey bucket while Darlene, smiling and pleasantly full of champagne, contentedly slept the night away.

9

Overtaken by the thrill of recalling Elijah's wedding feast, I overlooked telling about Harvey's return to Mother's that Fall, only to find Millwood comfortably occupying his bed and table space. Harvey could work up a torrid temper in no time at all, and when he found Millwood's bedroom slippers where his ought to be, he overheated quickly. Fortunately, as it turned out, neither Millwood nor Mother was at home when Harvey returned from Dahl Creek. Seeing what had happened in his absence, Harvey reddened and, with clenched fists, cornered a terrified Eureka in the kitchen, who blurted Millwood's transgressions without hesitation. In silence, Harvey picked up an empty two-pound Hills Brothers coffee carton and marched upstairs. Into the carton went Millwood's slippers, his shirts, undershirts, shorts, sox, shaving kit, his boots, every last part and parcel of Millwood's meager possessions. Down the stairs clomped Harvey, to the front door, where outside, on the top step, he placed none too gently the box containing Millwood's worldly goods.

Milwood had passed most of the afternoon with Paddy, but when he got home, carefully timed so not to miss supper, he recognized immediately his boots on top of the pile of belongings in the two-pound Hills Brothers coffee carton. Sadly, reluctantly, he knew it was over. Harvey was home from the creek.

10

And now, enough of wandering. Let me explain how we will proceed with Mother's treasured recipes. I propose first to discuss the ingredients, contents and manner of preparation of several of Mother's simplest gastronomic inspirations. After these have been completely understood and digested, we will move on to the more complicated and complex preparations for which dear Mother was most noted.

I trust now, that as you stand in your own cooking area, you can visualize that wonderful kitchen in Sawtooth House. Such a vision can only inspire you to greater things. So, gathering our skillets, pots, bagatelles, measuring spoons and worgels, with trembling hands we proceed!

As noted, we first will try four or five of the less complicated recipes. These will be:

    1. Fondue of marcassin with pilaf colthar.
    2. Croustarde de vino blautant with bourdin clafouti.
    3. Omelette a la muerre with roasted dauphines and mariweathers.
    4. Selle of lapis smothered in Bergian poularte glacee.
    5. Lyonaise of microbal with sauce bolvant fromale.

Before I proceed, an explanation of how Mother procured all the unique ingredients for her unusual recipes is in order. She was a great scavenger. As soon as the snow had left the tundra one could find Mother, basket in hand, searching for many of the pungent herbs and lysins which lent so much relish to her inspirations. Days were passed in this manner and, late each afternoon, she returned to her kitchen laden with wide varieties of her findings. These she carefully tended, dried, and stored for future use, for during the short summer months she was required to accumulate a supply sufficient to carry her through the long winter. No amount of trouble was too much. If she felt short of one necessity, off she would go, again and again, until her pantry was filled to surfeitude.

The same proved true of the pungent fluids she used so skillfully. Since tundrabuck and edsels were migratory, and grazed in the Nome area only during summer months, Mother was careful to procure a large supply of their milk. This she heated, boiled, condensed and purified for future use. Row upon row of these liquids, stored in magnacords, bottles and crandels, stood upon the shelves of her pantry. Each was carefully labled, as Mother would tolerate no mismatching of the ingredients she had gathered with such difficulty. It should be obvious that Mother had no lazy bones in her breasts.

One day Eureka, her natural curiosity piqued, asked Mother, "But how do you discover all these things–these herbs and lysins? How do you know where they are and whether they are good or bad?"

Mother's brow furrowed and we knew she was contemplating her answer.

"Necessity is the furlong of invention," she said.

The answer was so astute, so original, and had such a commanding tempo that it startled us, and we noted again how carefully Mother always chose her words.

Prybar

11

It has occurred to me that perhaps I should interrupt for a moment to complete the story of Prybar, as I dislike leaving anything unfinished.

Prybar was a lanky, rather unkempt man who always had a rumpled look about him. His shirts forever needed buttons, and large safety pins secured his suspenders. Usually he needed a shave pretty badly, and a professional haircut was something he had yet to experience. Several knots always were evident in his shoelaces where they had broken from time to time. Nevertheless, we all found Prybar to be a likable fellow and we enjoyed his company.

He had come to Nome in the late thirties with a bad case of gold fever and shortly thereafter secured a job on one of the Wild Plover Mining Co. dredges operating near town. He was single, having just been divorced by a second wife in Reno. He needed to get away, and since he recently had seen a movie based on a Rex Beach novel, the setting of which was Nome, he took steerage passage on the old steamship *Klondike* for the north country. He found himself in steerage because Sylvia, his former wife, had gone first class with the divorce. Prybar, or Austin, as he then was known, was left with his buttonless shirts and his safety pins and little else.

He landed in Nome on a bleak June day—one of those cold, gusty and wet days that only Nome and the Bering Sea, properly mated, can produce that time of year. To say he was shocked at Nome's shabby and neglected appearance would be an understatement. He was stunned. As Elijah was to do after him, he found unhappy accommodations at the Mukluk Inn. The room was small and barren, equipped with one straight chair with a mended leg, a cot with a mattress solid as a Nome rock, a battle-scarred, metal bedside table, and a bare light bulb shining dimly from the ceiling.

Archie had shown him to the room with a flourish reminiscent of the Waldorf and added, somewhat ceremoniously, "If you need anything, let me know." The door shut and Archie was gone. Prybar was stricken with a pang of homesickness. Even nagging and caustic Sylvia was better than this, but he would stay.

The next day Prybar presented himself to the personnel office of the Wild Plover Mining Co. Archie had told him that he had heard Wild Plover was hiring for the coming spring and summer season. Prybar filled out his application form with difficulty, for his education was limited. However, since he wrote under "Type of Employment Desired" the word "anything," anything is what he got. Dredge Number Two was working the old third beach line and the dredge master had called for a deck hand. It was work for any man with an able back and a none-too-inquiring mind. Prybar qualified.

He reported to the manhaul truck the next morning at six, rumpled as usual, and sleepy from a bad night on the Nome-rock bed. Seven or eight others also had reported and the manhaul took off, with a grinding clash of gears and a cloud of dust, over a bumpy and neglected gravel road toward the north of town. Soon he saw the dredge in the distance, a large boat-like contraption floating on its own pond. The bucket line descended in front and dug deeply, while out the back on a long conveyer belt the tailings, or gravel after it had been washed for gold, poured, forming small mountain ranges as the machine slowly swung back and forth. As the dredge dug in front and filled in behind, its own small lake moved with it.

As Prybar soon was to learn, water was the key element needed for operation of a gold dredge, for without water it could not function. A vast system of small canals, or ditches, as they were called, had been constructed over the years to bring water from the rivers miles inland to the various dredge ponds. It was a bigger operation than Prybar had imagined, as men were working everywhere.

Prybar noted ahead of the dredge a large area in which, every few feet, pipes with hoses attached were sticking from the ground. These, he learned, were the thaw fields, as the whole area, Nome included, was permafrost—permanently frozen ground—and before the dredge could dig, the ground must be thawed.

Well, on his first day at work, Prybar Plunkett got his name. It all occurred so fast no one knew at first really what had happened. Prybar's working companion was a fine young Eskimo lad from Shisapik named Danny Johnson. Danny was almost as new to the job as he was, and they took an instant liking to each other. As were most of the native people, Danny was friendly, open and anxious to learn. They got along splendidly.

Toward mid-afternoon and the end of their shift, Danny was ordered to loosen the line going from the dredge to the shore man in order that the dredge could move forward. Unaccustomed to the edge of the deck and unfamiliar with the manner in which the line was secured, Danny climbed over the railing to get a better look. Suddenly, with a terrified shout, he lost his footing and plunged flat-backed into the pond. Prybar, the only observer of the catastrophe, frantically called for help. Unfortunately, as with many native people, Danny could not swim. Prybar looked over the railing to see him thrashing about in the water and bobbing up and down like a float on a fish line. Shrieking for help, which failed to materialize, Prybar ran up and down the deck in a frantic effort to find something to throw to his struggling and drowning partner. Seizing what he saw first in a panic of helplessness, he grasped a huge iron prybar weighing at least seventy-five pounds and six feet long and hurled it over the railing to his gurgling friend.

By that time the entire dredge crew had been aroused, and all arrived on Danny's side of the dredge just in time to see the newest employee propel the immense iron bar into the pond. It struck the surface with an enormous splash some ten feet from the poor struggling Danny, and promptly disappeared in a flurry of scattering bubbles.

Quickly, the dredge master threw to Danny a life preserver which hung on the wall not ten feet from where he had fallen. He was pulled aboard, soaked and spewing water like a beached whale, but otherwise unharmed.

The men all looked at Austin Plunkett, doubled with laughter, and Austin was Prybar ever after.

12

Clover Blue found San Francisco to be a knock-rough city. In spite of what she considered to be wide reading on the subject of the world at large, she was wholly unprepared for what she found. For some days she wandered the streets, stopping at night at as inexpensive a hotel as she could find that had about it the aura of basic decency and cleanliness.

In the downtown area, everything she saw she could not have. In the trashy neighborhoods everything she saw she did not want. She watched round-eyed as limousines pulled to a stop in front of elegant Union Square shops, discharging aloof and worldly ladies, expensively dressed, expensively jeweled. She observed their meeting, the gushy greeting, the buss on the cheek, their disappearance into a world of money and influence she did not know.

After a few days of wandering, Clover Blue had rented a room at the Golden, a cheap hotel near the waterfront. It was more than plain, but basically clean and for the first time since leaving Nome it provided a place for her to call her own.

Clover Blue was surprised to find how quickly her savings were disappearing. Every meal, every night's lodging, reduced her limited assets more than she had anticipated. The solution, as each day passed, became more and more obvious. She needed a job sooner than she had planned. But how to find one and where? What she saw in the neighborhood of her hotel was limited to sleazy bars, cheap and dirty restaurants, and houses devoted to ladies of the night. She was determined to have none of these, particularly the latter, as it had been suggested to her that young and attractive women alone and in need of work always could find employment there.

When her financial situation had dwindled to four dollars, two dimes and a penny, she know she had to act. A "Waitress Wanted" sign in the front window of a small oriental restaurant found her attention, but she hesitated to go in. From across the street she watched the clientele enter and depart, mostly Chinese, mostly ill-clad, suggesting poverty equal to her own.

But there was no choice. She crossed the street, opened the door. The interior of the China Cup was noisy, crowded, steamy and smelled strongly of oriental spices. Clover Blue looked about her, hesitated, then drove herself forward. She pushed to the back, asked for the manager. She detested the place immediately, became aware of stares, that she was the object of discussion in a language she could not understand. Menus posted on the walls, now brown and stained with age, all were in Chinese characters. She could not find a word of English.

Before panic overtook her, a small oriental man came through swinging doors from the back, wiping his hands on a filthy white apron. He eyed her appreciatively. Clover Blue was beginning to perspire. He was of undecipherable age, round, plump, round face, round spectacles, round hands, round lips, round everything. Unconsciously, she stepped back, but was barred from movement by a table pushed close to the counter.

"You want job here?" the little round man asked,

emphasizing the "here." His eyes ran over her youthful and attractive figure.

She stammered, hardly knowing what she was saying. "I'm Eskimo from Nome, Alaska and I need a job."

"Eskimo? Eskimo?" he asked incredulously. "That's a new one!" Then he laughed.

She became aware that the hubbub of the restaurant had grown silent. All eyes were on her. She felt arrow-stares piercing her back.

"Sure, you work here." He leaned forward and fondled her breast a moment with fat round fingers. Saliva seemed loose in his mouth.

Clover Blue, startled by his over-familiar gesture, unconsciously folded her arms over her bosom. The crowd roared with laughter.

"You come ten o'clock, work nights." He leered at her suggestively.

Now it was only a matter of escape. "Yes," she blurted, "I'll come at ten o'clock and work nights." She wanted only to get away.

The experience at the China Cup had so terrified her, that for the rest of the day she was afraid to apply to any other place. She hurriedly had returned to the sanctuary of her small room. Inner strength would not allow tears.

Desperately she did not want to go back to Nome, at least not now. It raced through her mind that, if asked, Old Triple O doubtless would wire her the money. But no, she could not go back.

Although it was early evening and she had not had dinner, she removed her dress and climbed into the comfort of her narrow bed. Yes, in a way, Nome had been better than this. At least it had been familiar ground. It had been home.

Clover Blue suddenly was awakened by frantic beating on her hotel room door. Aroused from deep sleep, without ability to think clearly, she ran to the door and opened it. A dark-haired man pushed her aside, locked the door from the inside, quickly ran to the window, carefully parted the wilted curtains and surveyed the street below. Clover Blue, now fully awake, gasped, ran for her dress to cover herself. For the first time he turned to look at her.

"Don't worry, honey," he said. "I won't hurt you." He smiled, continuing to part the curtains to examine the scene at street level.

"I've got to wait it out," he said, turning to sit on a small stool near the window.

She examined him carefully. Well-dressed, dark even features, yes, handsome. Suddenly she realized she was not afraid, although she sensed she probably should be.

He lit a cigarette, inhaled deeply, said nothing. Finally, after half a smoke, he looked at her sitting on the bed holding her dress in front of her.

"You got a name?"

She did not answer, but surveyed him suspiciously.

"I'm going to be here a while. Why don't I look out the window while you put your dress on. You look kind of silly that way."

He turned, blew smoke through the partly raised window. Normal traffic noise filtered from the street below.

"Now, that's better," he said, turning really to look at her for the first time. He noted her slender, ripe young figure, tousled dark hair with highlights of auburn, but most of all her eyes, in the dim of the room, a strange, deep violet hue. "She really is beautiful," he thought.

She watched him, no longer suspicious or uneasy. She noticed his perfectly starched white shirt, expensive silk necktie, and French cuffs, which she had never seen before.

"You got a name?" he repeated.

"Clover Blue."

"You're kidding."

She remained silent.

He watched her, fascinated, the troubles that had brought him there somehow lost in the background.

"I'm Tony Conzarro," he said, getting to his feet. "I've made a couple of decisions right here. The first is, I'm going to marry you. The second, I'm never going to run from anyone again."

Tony was right on both counts. He did marry her three weeks later and, until the final moments, he never ran from anyone again.

Not long after Tony and Clover Blue were married, Tony drew her aside in the privacy of the study of his handsomely appointed penthouse apartment which they now shared, and stated some ground rules.

"I'm on the way up in the business," he explained. "I'm not going to tell you what the business is. I don't want you to hear it from me. Read the newspapers.

"It's important that you understand one thing," he went on. "Never once will I tell you anything about my affairs. I won't discuss any aspect of my business with you. I want you to have the protection of not knowing. Under no circumstances should you ever ask me or any of my associates about anything I do. Understand?"

Clover Blue nodded.

"Gee," Tony suddenly said, "to think I'm so lucky as to find you. I'm a sentimental guy. I love you so much I can't put it all together in my own mind. I can't seem to say what it means to me, what's happened with us, our getting together." He stopped, the shadow of a tear showing on his lower lashes.

Tony was right. He had played his gamble correctly. Only eighteen months after their marriage, he was named by the New York boss as manager of San Francisco operations.

Clover Blue could not believe the life they lived. Money was available for anything. She found the more money they had, the less she needed it. Everything was "taken care of." She learned that the ladies she had so envied in their limousines at Union Square were not top-list at all. Clover Blue went nowhere she did not wish to go. They came to her: dressmaker, jewelers, caterers, everyone.

Tony knew all the tricks. He was debonnaire, socially knowledgeable, understood the game. He realized the limitations of Clover Blue's background and decided she had to be educated to live in her new station in life. To this end Tony prevailed on Elena Goodman to instruct Clover Blue.

"You can be her Eliza," Tony said laughing, careful to be kind and understanding. Clover Blue had read and enjoyed Shaw. She knew to what he referred.

Elena, a sophisticate of San Francisco society, took hold with gusto. Clover Blue was an apt and eager student. Elena taught her how to dress with quiet elegance, the right colors, how to style her hair, to do her nails, her makeup. She taught her about cocktails—what and how much safely to drink, about table settings—which fork to use, which glass for what wine. She explained about the San Francisco people they would meet—who was important and who was not. In short, after only ten days of instruction, Clover Blue came out of a cocoon of self-doubt into a wonderful world of confidence, money and position.

At the time of their marriage, Tony Conzarro was widely known to the press as the man on the way up in the sphere of San Francisco's underworld. Photos occasionally were taken of the couple, although Tony hated publicity and made every effort to avoid press attention. Mostly, their life together remained unknown to the public. Tony had the money and influence to see to that. But the press was infatuated with Clover Blue so, in spite of all effort, she became a celebrity.

The one aspect of publicity that bothered Tony greatly was the continued inference that Clover Blue was privy to the intimate affairs of his business. In fact, Tony always had kept his word. Clover Blue knew nothing.

As years of their marriage passed, Clover Blue noticed subtle differences in her husband. From press reports she was aware that serious difficulties had developed in

Tony's business affairs. She knew Tony was thrusting for full leadership in San Francisco, independent of control of the New York boss. It worried her greatly, but as they had agreed, no discussion of these events took place between them. The closest Tony ever came to talking about his business was to tell her one day that he had put money aside for her future security.

"You should know," he said with forced nonchalance, "that over the past few years I have deposited money in an account for you. This is not dirty money. The government knows about it and all taxes have been paid. If anything should happen to me, my attorneys have full instructions."

Clover Blue forced the information from her mind, as she involuntarily did regarding any suggestion that harm could come to Tony. Thoughts of his deepening troubles were too devastating for her to dwell upon.

As the noose tightened on Tony in his efforts to break free, Clover Blue noticed that he had become secretive and withdrawn. He said, in passing, one day, "If anything happens to me, you must get out of San Francisco as soon as possible. Don't wait for anything, and I mean anything at all."

He laughed, kissed her, and she hugged him, finding it difficult to let go. She did not cry easily, but tears pushed into her eyes.

"But," he added, smiling the smile she knew so well, "nothing is going to happen." He lifted her chin to him, saw her tears, kissed her passionately.

"Tony, oh my God, Tony," was all she was able to say.

But Tony missed his call. When the chips finally were in and counted, New York held the aces. One by one, Tony's most influential, trusted and loyal associates drifted away from him. Finally, he heard that Chun Lin, boss of Chinatown's rackets, had pledged anew his loyalty to New York. It was the final devastating blow. Tony had lost.

He knew he had to talk to Chun Lin, that if he could,

he would convince him to change his mind. He realized the risks, and how the business operated. He had to take that chance. His driver took him to Chinatown, up the steep back street to where Chun Lin was careful to live, away from the glitter of Grant Street. Suddenly Tony desperately needed to talk to Clover Blue, to tell her again how dear she was to him, how deeply he loved her.

The black limousine pulled to the front of Chun Lin's dark and, from the exterior, unpretentious headquarters. Tony saw a phone booth a few feet down the street. He left the car, then he saw them. Two Chun Lin henchmen he recognized as friends, stepped from the darkened entrance of a nearby building. Tony began to run. He was aware that his own car immediately sped the scene. He turned, saw hard flashes of orange fire. Searing, violent, tearing pain scorched his body.

"Oh, God, Clover Blue!" he screamed loud enough for them to hear.

He spun, tried but could not run, buckled, fell, unbearable heat crossing and crisscrossing his body.

Then quietly, with last breath, he said, "Clover Blue," this time only for himself to hear.

13

But I have digressed, and we must return to Mother's gastronomic greatness. I have explained the manner in which she obtained some of her most prized ingredients and the patient care and vigilance she used to prepare and preserve them for future use. I expect no less from those seriously and truly interested in following her gourmet footsteps. So, out to the tundra and hills with your basket and pail! Soon, off we shall go into a wonderland of culinary delight.

Permit me to leave our main subject for a moment, however, as I should explain a bit about Archie Muller, the owner and operator of the Mukluk Inn. As round as he was high, with a shining bald pate and a ready smile, Archie labored day by day with his wife of twenty years, Pauline Esther. And Pauline Esther was what she insisted she be called. There was to be no "Pauline" or "Esther." Archie, who loved her dearly despite her sharpened tongue, had succeeded through the years in reaching a term of endearment to which she no longer objected. To him, she became Polly Esther. Although to most people pleasant enough, she always was a distant person who kept much to herself. There was something strange, almost synthetic about Polly Esther.

The Mullers had come to Nome in the depths of the depression on the old *Victoria*, which had patiently plied the waters from Seattle to Nome each summer season, year after year, for the Alaska Steamship Co. Archie had gone broke in San Diego the day after the stock market crash, and his formerly prosperous tourist boat business had gone on the rocks.

Why Nome? Pauline Esther had a sister living in Nome at that time and she had written that the depression had not hit Alaska as hard as other places, that mining was still prosperous, and that opportunities were reasonably good. Although, upon landing, they found sister Margaret's statements a bit exaggerated, the Mullers settled into the community without too much trouble.

Upon arrival in Nome in the mid-summer of 1930, Archie and Pauline Esther invested the meager remains of their finances in the purchase of the Mukluk Inn. The building was old, located at the far east end of town, and was one of the few destined to escape the great fire that devoured most of Nome in 1934. The former owner, Hal Moses, had lost interest in the business when the Lord had settled upon him late one night as he was sweeping dust from the hallway. The call to religion had been so real to Hal, that his main efforts henceforth were directed to the church. Thus when Archie and Pauline Esther took over, much needed to be done to bring the building and its interior to its present sub-standard condition.

The front end of the lower level of the Mukluk Inn had been given over to the Golden Egg saloon, which business accounted for the major source of income to the owners. The establishment was not originally called the Golden Egg, but the night before Archie and Pauline Esther were to go the office of the Territorial Clerk of Court to arrange transfer of the liquor license, Pauline Esther had a vivid dream in which a beautiful and bejeweled golden egg had danced before her eyes. So real was the dream, that she considered it to be an omen of good fortune. So, over Archie's mild objection, the saloon became the Golden Egg.

The Golden Egg was one of those old Nome liquor emporiums, now mostly gone from the city. The door from Front Street opened to a medium-sized room, worn wooden plank floor, a bar across the back and left side, and a row of tattered bar stools, the seat tops split here and there allowing the stuffing to protrude. Around the room were placed four or five decrepit, round wooden tables, with matching chairs, where cronies and other patrons could sit and play cribbage, panguingui or twenty-one. A juke box sat dusty in the corner, its colored panels dirty and occasionally cracked or broken. The oil heater, which functioned none too competently, rested against the far wall, its rusty chimney rising to exit the building at right angles through the outer wall. Over long years no one had changed the Golden Egg and none of the customers wanted it changed.

Archie and Pauline Esther knew the Mukluk Inn was not the prototype model for the American Hotel Owners' Association, but it seemed to fill a need in the community as a starting point for wanderers and lost souls, so many of whom found Nome, for one reason or another, the end of the path. As the years passed, they had met and helped many, including Prybar and Elijah, each of whom stayed to make his permanent home in Nome.

14

In the early forties Nome had a population of twenty-six hundred to twenty-eight hundred people, about two-thirds of whom were native or part native. Front Street, wide and imposing if not a sea of mud, maintained the usual small town businesses, but aside from commonplace items, the stock and trade noticeably was different.

Two mercantile stores competed for the town's grocery and general merchandising trade. The owner of the Cape Nome Mercantile Co., one Ezra Rifkin, carried such items strange to the neophite as walrus ivory tusks and caribou, seal, moose, reindeer, fox, wolf, wolverine and other furs. The meat department stocked such mysterious edibles as raw seal meat and seal oil, muktuk, whale blubber, seal liver, reindeer meat, dried walrus and oogruk. Also available were frozen, or fresh in season, spider crab, shee fish, dolly trout, rock fish, tomcod and white fish.

These strange delectables with their alien-sounding names often found their way to Mother's table, for as she was the mistress of gastonomic innovation, she always was willing to experiment with new discoveries. We must get back to Mother Sawtooth and her promised kitchen delights.

We have discussed to some considerable extent the ingredients needed truly to duplicate Mother's recipes. Now, before we begin, perhaps a word or two would be in order concerning the equipment necessary for success.

First, it strongly is recommended that an oil range of Mother's type be utilized. In this regard, a 1923 "Marvel Host" stove with a 1937 "Even All" oil converter should be acquired. Ask your local dealer for assistance. How else really to duplicate Mother's cleverness? For utensils, be sure to have readily available and at your finger tips, three or four two-thirds cup measuring spoons, a sturdy French baccarat, at least two quart-size mixing bowls, a gazebo with a wooden handle, a large roasting tray or mingel and the usual cups, saucers, floor mops and siphons. If the floor of your kitchen slants to the west, as did Mother's, you will need two small, hand-carved piranhas to level the legs of the mixing table.

Basic staples will consist of barley hilmer well-sifted, flour, both white and revoli, butter, or if you prefer you may substitute saffron olivine, as well as several kinds of hepars, cooking oils and bisques. Oh, yes! You will need some bottled spirits, for Mother was heavy with these at times. Recommended for ready use are wine, both wet and dry, brandy containing preserved findels, a choice grade of Italian bourbon, scotch if you like it, and rose-tinted argoyle alcohol.

On one occasion, a friend of Mother's asked her how she accomplished the gathering of so many fine and unique utensils and supplies to assist her with her kitchen creations. Mother reflected for a moment and answered, "The proof of the pudding is in the rubbing."

What a superb reply! Only Mother Sawtooth could have originated such a well-turned and considered phrase.

We all carefully noted what she had said.

15

As indicated earlier, Nome did not have, and could not have, a municipal water system. The perpetually frozen ground, called permafrost, upon which the town was built, allowed for no buried pipes. Thus, another method to satisfy the thirst of the community had to be found.

Louis Napoleon owned and operated the Nome Water Delivery Service. He was a displaced Frenchman, having arrived in Nome under mysterious circumstances in the early days of the gold rush. He never found his way home again. It was rumored that Louis was an escaped felon from the justice of France, but no one could substantiate that claim. In any event, he settled into the life of the community without difficulty and became the Nome water delivery man.

In the first years, Louis operated the business from a horse-drawn tank wagon, a bedraggled team of old cast-offs pulling the heavily laden wagon about town for the usual deliveries. But as soon as it was feasible, he converted to a tank truck and the old horses were sent to their overdue reward in equine heaven, where grass is always succulently green and all the tank wagons suffer broken axles. Louis had never developed a close relationship with his beasts of burden as, for example, Cletus Strong had done with his revered old Prince. So the parting was on equal terms—good riddance on either side.

When he was forty years old, some fifteen years after arrival in Nome, Louis married Nina Langley, the daughter of an early-day prospector. Nina was no raving beauty, and was well on her way to permanent maidenhood when Louis took an interest in her. She was a robust woman with a quick wit, solid background, and a good business head. She was just what Louis needed, as simple arithmetic in the nature of record keeping and billing left him flustered and confused. Before Nina, every eraser on every pencil that Louis owned was worn to a scratchy nubbin. Louis claimed that numbers in France were different from numbers in America, and he simply could not contend with the difference.

Nina kept the books, sent out the monthly statements, recorded delinquencies, and so another French-American crisis was averted. There were few delinquencies with Nina in charge, however, as it was well known about town that Nina would "cut off your water" if regular payment was too long in arriving.

Louis had an assistant who worked for him all through the years. His name, which he detested from earliest comprehension of what his parents had done to him, was Reginald Merton Rivers. Of course the young boy, forthwith, was known as "Reggie," which he hated, and as far back as he could remember he was taunted by schoolmates for being a sissy. Reggie was no sissy. Even as a lad he was stocky, well-built, muscular, and able to defend himself. Although the teasing usually ended when Reggie trounced a few of his tormentors, those victories did nothing to dispel the hatred he had for his name. Fortunately it was Reggie's father who came to the rescue. Noting the sturdy build of the young boy, he began to call him "Rocky." So blessed, the name stuck and from that day on, he was Rocky Rivers.

Each morning except Sunday found Louis and Rocky at the Bourbon Creek well house, little gas pump chugging away, filling the large water tank strapped to the truck bed. A full load required most of an hour, so the two sat on wooden apple creates, each pretty much with his own thoughts, as conversation was difficult over the piping little motor. Louis puffed on a nearly ever-present cigar while Rocky munched spicy gum drops, a well developed addiction. When the sound of the rushing water told practiced ears the tank was nearing capacity, the pump was silenced with a flick of the gas line shutoff valve and the two men were off for the day's endeavor.

It really was inevitable that Louis Napoleon, operator of Nome's water delivery service, was to become known to the community as "Water Lou." The origin of this most appropriate nickname was lost in time and few, if any, of the town's citizens knew Water Lou's real name. Thus, over the years, Water Lou and Rocky Rivers, much to the town's amusement, plodded their daily rounds, bucket after bucket dumped into the small outdoor receptacle on the side of each house, from whence a pipe led to the storage tank within. Water was thirty cents a five-gallon bucket. The system kept Nome from thirst and bathlessness, and provided a comfortable living for Water Lou and Rocky Rivers.

Each home had been provided a large white card with a big black "W" printed in the center. The card was placed in the front window, with a tag appended indicating the number of buckets needed. It all worked very well as long as the homeowner accurately estimated his needs. If too much was ordered on the front window card, the result was an inundation of corresponding proportions for which Water Lou, as owner of the business, would assume no responsibility.

Mother Sawtooth was especially fond of the pair. Her active kitchen utilized more than the average amount of water, and she appreciated their reliability. Often, when delivery had been completed and Mother's storage tank was comfortably full, she would invite Water Lou and Rocky Rivers into her kitchen for freshly-baked nizzle rolls or claynor doughnuts. The latter were made with little known and seldom used blue tundra yeast, carefully gathered by Mother each Spring. The peculiar yeast gave the puffy, irregular doughnuts a strong blue color and a strange taste, resembling crewley nuts, startling to the novice taster.

For their part, Water Lou and Rocky Rivers looked forward to the almost daily delivery to Sawtooth House. Usually, they carefully timed their arrival near eleven in the morning, an hour they knew that active Mother Sawtooth would have her baking done and the kitchen would effervesce of fresh produce from her oven. They enjoyed talking to her, remembered her wise counsel, and generously consumed the always-delicious result of her labors.

It is my profound hope to include in this book the recipes for Mother's nizzle rolls and claynor doughnuts as well as many other spectacular creations from her kitchen.

16

A pause is in order here for a few lines about Nome's elite. It just occurred to me that, except for Mother Sawtooth herself, I have mentioned no one who could be so categorized. I think readily of Maynard Willard who owned the local shipping and lighterage company. He had come to Nome from Buffalo as a young man, fresh from a disastrous high school career during which he had passed two years as a member of the Senior class. Maynard had two younger brothers, both of whom, unfortunately, carefully and openly outshone him in nearly his every endeavor. Thus, when Maynard at last graduated from high school following his unique five-year course, and an opportunity arose for him to join a second-cousin who owned a hardware store in Walla Walla and was in need of a novice clerk, Maynard's father readily agreed and prudently provided a one-way railroad ticket for his eldest son's western adventure.

Three months in Walla Walla and a hopelessly confused inventory, the result of Maynard's talent as a hardware salesman, convinced his second-cousin that Maynard should move on to brighter things. Realizing that in the long run it would be less taxing on his hypertension, as well as his bank account, to assist Maynard on his way financially, the good but frustrated man presented Maynard with a continuing one-way rail ticket to Seattle plus thirty dollars in cash. A good pat on the back and a prod toward the waiting railway coach got Maynard on his way, as his second-cousin stated, "to Seattle, Queen City of the Pacific Northwest, the gateway to Alaska where opportunity beckons."

It was no accident that brought Maynard to Alaska. He had always been fascinated by tales of the gold rush, then not long past, and in fact, during his school days he once had written an English paper about Alaska, which his teacher actually had commended. He remembered reading about Fairbanks and Nome and the big gold strikes at the turn of the century.

Upon arriving in Seattle that rainy November day in 1921, Maynard marked his course to the north. Embarking for Seward, an Alaskan port free of ice all year around, he made his way from there to Fairbanks on the chugging and recently finished Alaska Railroad. The trip was dreary and cold, for the cars were heated only by small and inefficient coal stoves at either end, seldom tended by the conductor.

Fairbanks in November and December was not to Maynard's liking. The days were frigid and dark and it seemed the inhabitants rarely moved from the shelter of their homes. Snow drifted and piled high everywhere. Forty below zero he found to be normal, with colder temperatures not unusual. Because of his "experience" in the hardware store, the details of which Maynard was careful not to divulge, he was hired as a clerk at the Far North Grocery and Supply Co. He survived the winter but barely, it seemed to him, and when the first drops of water dripped from the eaves the following Spring he determined to seek his northern fortune elsewhere.

Saying his goodbyes to his employer, as he had been well treated, Maynard embarked again south to Seward on the now-familiar Alaska Railroad. He had discovered something, too, in Fairbanks which changed his opinion of himself and proved most fortuitous to his future. He found that, when properly instructed, he had mathematical talent. He seemed to be a natural bookkeeper and accountant.

17

Alas, I must return to Sawtooth House and to the real purpose of this book. I have wandered. But to recall Mother's adroitly beautiful table, set with her fine silverplate and crockery, veritably loaded to the margins with gastronomic prizes, invites memories of other happenings and other persons. So perhaps you will forgive me if I deviate from our main subject to finish the story of Maynard Willard.

But first, dear cook and patient reader, let me outline and list those things which it is my understanding will be necessary for our first noble culinary quest. This, of course, is the fondue of marcassin with pilaf coltahr. And what a grand and imposing concoction it is! I recall Mother, smiling tearfully as she entered from that precious kitchen, for she was emotional about her creations, a large morika of fondue of marcassin steaming in her clever and aptitudinal hands. Following, of course, came Eureka with the pilaf, happy and blossomed to be a part of it all. The fondue must not be overdone and one must have an aluminum and cobalt miroka for best results. It is served tepid and hot into individual resel shells, the pilaf as a bountiful foundation.

When the fondue had been finished and we all sat back nodding our heads in grateful appreciation, I asked Mother how she always could be sure of such wonderful results.

Mother laughed, thought deeply, and wisely stated, "In this world, nothing is certain but death and taxes." We all recognized an unforgettable tempo to that answer and we were impressed, as usual, by her originality and creativeness.

I have told you something of the beginning of the fondue recipe, and these hints of things to come should whip every tooth in your body to an expectant lather. But, as promised, I will pause here to continue the story of one of Nome's real elite, Maynard Willard.

The return trip from Fairbanks to Seward took Maynard through the tiny railroad town of Anchorage. He got out of the coach briefly to stretch his legs and look about as he was searching for a new location in which to establish himself. Since the dusty little town exhibited little evidence or promise of any future, he reentered the railroad car for the continuation of the trip to Seward. Maynard considered himself to be an excellent judge of communities and the portent their futures exhibited.

Upon arrival in Seward, Maynard felt with some justification that he was back where he had started. In the newly-constructed railway depot he examined a large map of Alaska that was pinned to the freshly painted wall. He had been to Fairbanks and had failed. The other town he had discussed in his English paper, was Nome. With some difficulty he located it on the map, for his mind's eye always placed that city too far to the north. Inquiry revealed that a ship was to arrive in Seward, bound for Nome, the following week. Maynard booked passage.

His arrival in Nome was inauspicious. Landing from the barge which had carried the passengers ashore, Maynard caught his shoe on a protruding nail and spread-eagled upon the dock. More embarrassed than injured, he sheepishly proceeded into town followed by the bemused stares of his fellow passengers, one of whom was Orville Oscar Osterman, returning home.

Since Maynard had managed to save a few dollars from his job in Fairbanks, and shortly before he left that city he received a panicky letter from his father in which a crisp fifty dollar bill had been enclosed, he was able to escape the usual Nome first days at the Mukluk Inn. He took instead, a small, but comfortable room at the Bonanza Hotel and set out to see the town.

Dinner at the Surefine Grill brought him the information that O. O. Osterman, "Old Triple O" as he locally was known, was in need of an assistant and bookkeeper at the dock and lighterage office, as Remus Sheppard again had battled with his argumentative wife and departed the country without notice.

The interview with Old Triple O was brief and to the point.

"I want a man who is reliable and a good bookkeeper," he stated. I'm an old man and my eyes don't do well anymore. Can you handle the job?"

Maynard swallowed hard, bouncing his Adam's apple up and down like a ball on a rubber band, and stated that he could.

Thus began his association with Old Triple O and the Nome Storage and Lighterage Co., which was to last a lifetime.

"I know everyone calls me Old Triple O behind my back," Osterman announced to Maynard the following day. "I don't care. My father called me Triple O when I was a boy, before Nome was on the map. You call me Orville."

Maynard took to his work like a caribou to moist green tundra grass. He loved the excitement of the waterfront, the coming and going of tugs and barges, and the Bering Sea, restless and blue-gray in summer and white and frozen calm in winter. He grew to admire and like gruff old Orville, who had come to Nome's tent city in '99 as a stampeder from the Klondike, and who had stayed to grow wealthy in the business of supply and transport for the miners, rather than to mine himself.

As the years went by, Maynard's relationship with Orville became close, and the latter depended heavily upon him in the operation of the business. Orville paid him handsomely, for he was able to do so without strain upon his own limited needs or those of the company.

One day, nearly ten years after Maynard had come to Nome, Orville came into his office.

"I had a birthday last week, you know," Orville announced abruptly. "I just turned eighty-six and I've got to quit. If you want the business you can have it. I've got few needs, and only relatives I've never even seen. It's no gift," he went on, "I want thirty thousand for everything."

The price, indeed, was fair, as the business was worth much more.

Although the depression was hitting the nation with furor, Alaska, particularly Nome, was surviving well. Gold mining prospered, labor was plentiful, and distance and isolation to some extent divorced the Alaska Territory from the bitter economic impact felt in the Lower 48.

Maynard accepted Orville's offer. When his father had died six years earlier Maynard unexpectedly had inherited nearly seventeen thousand dollars. From his salary he had been able to save, so it was with the aid of a small loan from the Miners and Merchants Bank of Nome that he easily raised the money for the purchase.

On December 31, 1931, when the homes of Nome were bright with holiday sparkle and the new year was greeted with happiness and confidence, Maynard became the sole owner of the Nome Storage and Lighterage Co.

18

The holidays were great days at Mother Sawtooth's, and Christmas was the most memorable time of all. Through the years, Mother had collected decorations to bring holiday cheer to the walls and rooms of Sawtooth House. Great garlands of ellenrude hung from the ceilings and were draped about the rooms from sill to sill. Mistletoe was everywhere, the result of Harvey's endeavor, as he loved to catch Mother, Shirley, or Eureka unaware.

Since the Nome area is treeless tundra, "les arbes de noel," as Mother liked to call our Christmas trees, were difficult to procure. For this purpose, Harvey and I hitched my dog team and mushed the some fifty miles to the east, where the timber line ended. There we chose a nice spruce and a bushy senwar and returned triumphantly to Mother's, where tinsel, colored balls, streamers, itanian corbonos, and lights were affixed. The house was a happy sight, if somewhat overdone, with its garlands, trees, wreaths, bells and dangles, but Mother's presence and cheery personality made it all endurable.

Christmas dinner, of course, was a delight and the apex of the year. Aside from her usual boarders, Mother always asked other good friends in the community to join us. Thus the dinner was a gala affair, with so many expectants filled with expectation crowded around the table. Certain dishes and preparations had become traditional as the years had passed. The table was leaden with food.

Always, Mother began the meal with generous servings of mandolin of caracara seasoned with spices and granolas. Next, of course, she served one of her favorite soups, rezin of potage with grunions parmici. I should say here, somewhat parenthetically, I suppose, that we surely will get to these esophagal delights, and others, so I do hope you are prepared to proceed. After the rezin of potage came a lovely salad of canned vegetables including lettuce, parchisis, radishes, pelliwinkles and powdered grimlets. These all were tossed together with a light oil and barkley dressing and delightfully seasoned with tundra moss and lichens.

Now, by all that is right and noble, a blare of trumpets should sound—for through the kitchen door came Mother, carrying her antique petulla, upon which sat a perfectly roasted and browned holiday bush turkey, complete with hipple dressing and stuffed creaton apples. It was a sight for sore molars! Harvey did the honors of proposing a toast to Mother, after Eureka had finished pouring a nice moist rosé wine into our cups. Harvey rose to his feet, cleared his throat, rapped for quiet, raised his cup and, looking directly into Mother's eyes, toasted her beautifully.

"Here's kelp in your propeller," he said.

All cups held aloft, we drank to Mother's health and to the produce of her kitchen. She was widely pleased.

Harvey carved the turkey, using the traditional antique Christmas cleaver that had been in Mother's family for over ten years. We all sat spellbound as he expertly served each plate. Then the sauces, condiments and relishes were passed, followed by Mother's light yeast and baking powder rolls. The meal was bountifully delicious and filling, and we all anticipated and looked forward eagerly to dessert and the courses to follow.

As we ate we all sat silently as Eureka tenderly sang "Oh, Holy Night" in Eskimo, accompanying herself on the magnoharp. It was very touching, especially her high notes.

Dessert was Mother's famous Eskimo ice cream—a wondrous combination of seal tallow, huckleberries, Moravian pistals and sisal. Coffee royale de puce followed, after which we all repatriated to the living room for a gift exchange. I received a lovely korgan lamp, shaped in the form of a duckwhittle with an electric bulb in its open mouth. It was charming.

When all the gifts had been opened and the coffee royale de puce consumed, we sat about the room complacent and satisfied. Again, the conversation turned to the sumptuous holiday repast that had been provided.

"How do you do it, and with so little assistance?" someone asked Mother. She was deep in thought. Then she answered.

"God helps them that helps themselves," she said.

As usual, the perfect answer. We were impressed by the originality of Mother's verbal inventiveness.

19

I should in all fairness complete the story of Maynard Willard. I was carried away by the memory of that captivating Christmas dinner.

By 1943, Maynard was preparing to take a third wife. The first had fallen in love with a local doctor and had departed unexpectedly. The second, when she arrived in the Spring of 1942, had decided, upon seeing Nome for the first time, that the city already had been bombed by the Japanese and everyone was keeping it a secret. She returned to Seattle on the next boat.

Maynard's third wife, Sheila, had been much-married herself. Quite a bit younger than Maynard, she was a sleek brunette with curves enough to draw the eye of any passing male. Sheila wanted money and security, and Maynard wanted a sensuous and chic wife. It was love at second glance, and they were married by the dottery old U. S. Commissioner in the elegant apartment Maynard had built above his offices, not long after the old company buildings he had inherited from Orville had been lost in the great fire of 1934.

On that September morning the fire had started small enough, as all fires do. Harry Hobart's still in the old Golden Gate Hotel had blown up and, with a beating of wet towels and rugs, Harry had almost managed to get the blaze under control. But the flames escaped him and with the aid of a strong wind off the sea, a holocaust soon developed which was far beyond the abilities of Nome volunteer firemen to control. The flames leapt from the Golden Gate to the large Oddfellows Hall next door and Maynard, watching from a window of his office nearby, knew all was lost. Quickly, he gathered his important accounting books and the photographs of his mother and father from his desk, and headed for the door. The tinder-dry old wooden buildings burned like tissue with the aid of the wind, and so fast had the fire progressed, he barely escaped the building. The narrow little streets and the overhang of the buildings provided a path for the flames which was impossible to block. Thus, from the safety of the beach, Maynard watched the quaint old gold rush Nome he had known so long and grown to love so dearly, disappear in a flurry of fire, smoke and sparks.

The cinders of the old town barely were cool before rebuilding plans had begun. Since the fire occured in mid-September, the last ship of the season already had left Seattle for Nome. Lumber, building supplies of all kinds, fixtures, everything was needed and needed badly before the sea froze over for the long winter months. The only portion of the original town still standing was the peripheral crescent of the outskirts. The entire business district and the center of the city were gone.

Telegraphic communication with the outside world was soon reestablished by the U. S. Army-operated Alaska Communications System. After a short period of indecision, the Alaska Steamship Co. agreed to dispatch a relief ship, which arrived in mid-October, loaded to the gunwales with food and necessities needed to rebuild the town. Temporary shelters quickly went up in order that the homeless could survive the winter. Maynard constructed a one-room shelter in which he endured the winter in the company of several bachelor employees. The building proved nearly impossible to heat, but somehow they survived to greet Spring's first flock of snow geese with optimism and confidence.

The town was replatted. Gone was winding, narrow old Front Street, to be replaced by a wide, straight thoroughfare. Maynard rebuilt as quickly as possible his warehouses, storage buildings, garages and offices. It was the latter that intrigued him, for the second story was to be his living quarters—a new, lovely and elegant apartment with great windows overlooking the Bering Sea. No more fires, determined Maynard, and the office-apartment complex was built of reinforced cement—a concrete example to others of his confidence in the future of Nome.

20

I have ranged far from Mother's kitchen stove, but I have good news. Recently, while Mother was making her widely-regarded saute of wild mountain sheep strawberries with seschel and chervil, I noted, by careful observation, most of her cherished recipe. So let us start there.

In your largest cast iron frying skillet, saute in kelton oil over medium heat, finely chopped onions and seschel. Stir constantly until the seschel has dissolved and the onions are multicolored. Set aside and allow to cool until lukewarm. It is presumed that you have arranged with several hunters to bring you the small, skin pouch of the ram containing the "strawberries." This is a vitally important step, as rams are loathe to stand still for direct procurement. Now, don't be squeamish! Remove the two "strawberries" from the pouch and discard the latter, although, if you are the type to do so, once properly tanned, you will have an excellent tobacco or snoose pouch. Well, that was rather a digression, so on with the recipe.

Now the marinade is to be prepared, for we must dispose of the strong and pungent wild sheep odor before proceeding. Into three cups of kelton oil and two-thirds cup of white swamp vinegar, add enough turgin and barlow pod to turn the mixture dark brown. Allow to settle. Then add one tablespoon of sugar and four or five drops of doffelseed extract, just enough to return the marinade to its original color and consistency. Into this entrancing mixture, drop the "strawberries," being especially careful not to splash any of the mixture on your good counter top. Allow to stand one to two hours. If the marinade foams, remove the delicacies with a flat stainless steel okol spoon in order that the concoction can aerate. Do not rinse foam down your kitchen drain.

When you are satisfied that the "strawberries" are completely marinated, arrange them on a large stoneware platter and surround with pungent kuvel and pindon leaves. Pour the remaining liquid over all and prepare for a feast sufficient to satisfy even the most discriminating gourmet. You will find it a rare occurrence that any guest forgets this magnificent offering.

21

At this point we were interrupted, but I assure you every effort will be made to procure many of Mother's other tantalizing recipes. These surely will be forthcoming. Arne had come in with the mail, which had arrived by air from Fairbanks that morning.

I should explain that the early forties were years of the very beginning of organized commercial aviation in the Nome area. Although bush pilots had flown the region some before, Pan American Airways was pioneering the Alaska routes on a scheduled basis. Actually, because of the war, Pan American had been taken over by the Navy, but the company still served Fairbanks and Nome from Seattle on a limited basis with its small and silver sleek Electras.

Receiving air mail in those days was a novel thrill, as was flying itself. Before the airplane, mail was received in Nome by boat only during the summer months or, rarely, in the winter by dog team from Fairbanks—a trek requiring four to six weeks.

The mail contained another letter to Mother from Kirk. This was the second in as many months and quickly she put aside her spoons and divets with somewhat unsteady hands. The letter carefully read, Mother tucked it into her ample bosom without comment, as she appeared both troubled and pleased.

I never had met Kirk, but I was told he had preceeded Harvey in Mother's attentions. He was described as a tall, handsome, out-going fellow with steel-gray hair and a slender, well-kept figure. Everyone sensed that Mother had been particularly fond of him. However, when Kirk had left Nome three years before, Harvey had been waiting in the pantry, so to speak, and Mother seemed quickly to forget that Kirk existed.

Kirk had been employed by Maynard Willard for a number of years as waterfront foreman. Kirk had been a capable and trustworthy employee, and when he decided to return to California to aid the war effort by working for one of the large shipbuilding firms, Maynard could not in good conscience attempt to deter him. He had said his goodbyes to Mother in the privacy of their bedroom, quickly and on short notice. The last boat of the season had sailed that night for Seattle, and all assumed that with it, Kirk had sailed from Mother's life.

Kirk and Paddy O'Brien had been good friends, and Kirk had spent a considerable amount of time at The Glue Pot although he was by no means a heavy drinker. Nor, strangely, was Paddy. They simply enjoyed each other's company, hunted and fished together when time allowed, and argued politics and, on occasion, religion, but the arguments never were serious and did not result in hard feelings between them.

Paddy O'Brien had been born and raised in Butte, Montana, of Irish immigrant parents. His father had worked the copper mines under the "richest hill on Earth" for Anaconda Copper, and had died in a mine accident when Paddy was fourteen. His mother was left with Paddy and two younger children. She was a strong and determined woman, but of little education, so she turned to housework to support herself and her children. Paddy had worked with her when not required to be in school, for she insisted he finish high school no matter what the sacrifice.

In summer, Paddy had mowed the lawns and tended the gardens of Butte's wealthy, and in winter he shoveled the walks and cleared the ice from steps and porches. With his mother, he had walked the thirteen blocks to West Platinum Street where the large homes stood, stately and imposing, their interiors as foreign to him as their owners, as always they paid his mother for his work.

When Paddy had finished high school he was aware that Butte held little future for him other than the mines, and he wanted to find broader horizons. His mother sensed correctly his restlessness and his need to find a life elsewhere, as she did not want Paddy to go into the mines. "Pit College," they called it, as it was understood that once enrolled with pick and lantern, graduation seldom came. Thus, though it tugged her heart to do so, she encouraged him to leave Butte to seek his chances elsewhere.

It was not that Paddy disliked mining or found the work distasteful. He was fascinated with its run-of-the-luck nature, but his father's death deep inside the mountain had haunted him. He disliked the thought of being under the earth, so trapped in the event of an emergency.

It was these thoughts that brought Paddy to think of gold, for he knew enough to recognize that, for the most part at least, gold mining was a top-of-the-ground pursuit. The romance of Nome and the history of the Big Strike on Anvil Creek were well known to him, as he always had been a reader. Since mining in general fascinated him, he had read everything he could find in the Butte Public Library about Nome and its gold.

When he told his mother that June day in 1913 that he wanted to go to Nome, Alaska, she looked at him incredulously. She would not have been more astonished had he said he was going to The Congo to convert the natives to Buddhism. Although she surely had heard of Nome and, as a matter of fact remembered hearing Paddy speak of it from time to time, in her mind it was not a place to which anyone ever really went. But when she realized he was serious, with secret reluctance she gave him her blessing and fifeen dollars of the money saved from the days of his high school labors.

Three days later he was aboard a coach of the *Olympian*, a cross-country train operated by the Chicago, Milwaukee and St. Paul Railroad, bound for Seattle. Paddy's one promise to himself was that as soon as he was working, no matter what the sacrifice to his personal needs or comfort, he would send money on a regular basis to his mother. This vow was never broken, for as long as she lived, each month she received a note from Paddy with currency enclosed. It made her life easier and she loved him all the more for it, as she was able, after a while, to cut the days she worked from six to five.

As we all did, Paddy arrived in Nome a total stranger to his surroundings. No amount of explanation or reading can convey to the unfamiliar what Nome is like. This remote city is not for the impotent or unnerved. A mixed collection of wooden buildings holding to the beach, dirt streets, days of ever sunlight in summer and near always dark in winter, isolated by nature's seasonal ice packs and the freezing Bering Sea.

Before the airplane, transportation to the west coast of the Lower 48 was limited to the three or four ships of summer, the first arriving near the end of June, and the last departing in early October. It was seldom that the ice loosened its grip before mid-June, and rarely did a vessel risk the Bering Sea after October 15th. By then, mush ice was forming on the beach, the pilings, and the water edge of ships. Soon the mush ice would solidify and the sea became a great plain of white as far as vision allowed. Sky and water joined and could not be marked one from the other.

22

Paddy found gold, but it was not his. To his amazement, rows of shiny golden bricks were stacked in the front window of the Miners' and Merchants' Bank for all to see. Millions had been taken from Nome's sand and dirt and this was a part of it. At first he thought it to be a joke, but later learned the bricks were real and waiting to be packed for shipment to the Lower 48 on the next boat.

Paddy examined the stacked bricks carefully. This is gold, real gold, he told himself. Never had he expected to see that much in one place at one time. He was fascinated to learn that when a large gold shipment such as this was prepared for transfer by barge to the waiting ship in the roadstead, certain novel precautions were taken.

First, the bricks were weighed and inventoried, then packed in secure wooden crates bound tightly with steel bands. But most interesting of all to Paddy, when placed on the barge, the relatively small but extremely valuable boxes were loaded last, placed squarely on top of all other cargo. Securely fastened to each crate was a coiled, strong rope with a large float attached to the end. If the barge met disaster between shore and ship, and such happening was not wholly unknown in the rough and unpredictable waters of the Bering Sea, the float led searchers to the location of the packing crates so they safely could be rescued from the bottom.

In a way, Paddy's dream came true. He found work above ground with a sluicing crew on a tributary of the Goodhope River, near the small settlement of Deering, north and west of Nome. The work was difficult, the hours long, but he loved every moment of it. It was a good season for his employer, Med Davis. Hydraulic hoses brought the embankment down and the gravel and water washed over the riffles of the sluice boxes. At the end of each week, "clean-up" came, and the crew crowded about to see the accumulation of gold. Usually the yield was good and Med was pleased, as he knew he was working rich ground. But once in a while, for no apparent reason, the result of the week's work was disappointing. Analysis was futile, for the nuggets and flour gold kept well their secrets.

When Paddy was twenty-four, some six years after his arrival in Nome, he met and married Florrie Ogden. She had arrived only that summer with her parents, her father being the new superintendent for Wild Plover Mining Co. Florrie and her parents lived in a most- pleasant apartment on the third and top floor of the big mining company building. It was the tallest structure in town.

Paddy had gone to work for Wild Plover the second year he was in Nome. His spark and ambition were recognized, and he became assistant warehouseman, a postion he much enjoyed. Florrie bore him two sons, Michael and Steven, and a daughter, Mary, a beautiful child with dark hair and brown eyes as large as the buttons on Paddy's good winter coat.

By 1938 Paddy had progressed to chief warehouseman for Wild Plover, but a restlessness had seized him. So, when the opportunity came to buy the Glue Pot, he broached the subject to Florrie. He was forty-five years old, and the children had grown and were finding lives of their own. Paddy always had met people well and he knew he would enjoy the contacts of a business downtown. At the warehouse on the north edge of the city next to the company powerhouse, he was isolated and rarely saw anyone other than company employees.

Florrie did not like the idea of getting involved in the liquor business. She was suspicious of where it might lead, and with some justification, as Mike the Turk, who wanted to sell the saloon, had through the years become a tragic and hopeless alcoholic. Though not an old man, Mike long since had left most of his liver in the bottom of whisky glasses at the

Glue Pot, and he knew he had to give up the business. The saloon always had been a good money maker, and the possibility of increasing his income appealed to Paddy. He wanted to be able to do more than retire on the limited income his years at Wild Plover would provide.

They reached a compromise. Florrie agreed that Paddy could buy the Glue Pot on two conditions: The first was that she never was to be required to take an active part in the operation of the bar and second, with unfortunate Mike the Turk in mind, that Paddy not drink hard liquor while tending bar or on the premises of the Glue Pot.

It was the second condition that disturbed Paddy, not that he was a drinker, but he knew from experience in the downtown saloons that it would be very difficult not to consume a drink now and then when a well-meaning customer wanted to buy, or "timbered" the house.

It was Kirk who arrived at the solution. An answer so simple, yet it had eluded both Florrie and Paddy. "Drink apple juice," Kirk explained. "A glass of apple juice looks just like whiskey and water and who will know the difference?"

It worked. And so it was that Paddy kept apple juice behind the bar and partook of this delicious but fraudulent drink when there was no other out. As time passed he grew more than weary of apple juice, but he kept his promise to Florrie, and that was most important.

One might think that Kirk should have purchased the Glue Pot, for he had another suggestion for Paddy which proved invaluable to the resounding success of the business after Paddy took over.

"As far as the bar is concerned, become a character," Kirk advised. "People love to be around a bartender who has a reputation for amusing eccentricities."

Paddy took Kirk's advice and developed a saloon character which greatly differed from his norm. He became the lovable gruff, reminiscent of early Nome days, and dressed the part with white shirt, string bow tie, sleeve garters, red vest and nugget chain. In spite of the fact that Florrie mildly complained that kissing Paddy was like kissing a scrub brush, he grew a magnificent handlebar mustache which became famous throughout the community and, if nothing else, brought the new and curious to the bar. He developed the natural ability of his Irish heritage to remember good stories and to tell them well. In short, Paddy's Glue Pot became the most popular watering place in Nome. As long as Paddy was behind the bar, the establishment was well-patronized.

Paddy ran a good business. He never allowed the drunken or the vulgar to remain for long. Entertainment, though limited, was bright and amusing, and always within the bounds of good taste.

The success of the Glue Pot under Paddy's management was rewarding, as within a few years of taking over, he was a wealthy man with money well invested for his and Florrie's retirement.

23

During these years Mother Sawtooth and Sawtooth House were, of course, important segments of the community. The table set at Mother's had gained renown beyond Nome, and frequently room was made for visitors on special occasions. The greatness of Mother's culinary art weighed heavily upon her from time to time and every now and then she appeared unresponsive and cheerless. Such was not her nature, for Mother's talent allowed her to tolerate those of us less gifted.

On one occasion a visitor, who had partaken of Mother's sumptuous cravat of wild willow fowl with molded parlous croquettes and rice, asked her if her fame and greatness weighed upon her. Mother pondered the question and we sensed she was thinking.

"To be great is to be misunderstood," Mother answered.

The reply was so pertinent, so well put and original, that involuntarily we all applauded. The visitor was taken aback, but we knew a sense of Mother Sawtooth's originality and true greatness had been imparted.

Shirley and I broke up in mid-August. She never had overcome her fascination with the theater and, in spite of all that I could tell her, she wanted to continue her study of the dance. She had been careful not to miss any Friday or Saturday showing of a Hollywood musical at the Dream Theater, and I knew she visualized herself in the arms of a handsome dancing partner as the cameras rolled. It was not that she lacked beauty, for she had excellent features. The truth was that she ever seemed to be heavy on her feet and I could not foresee her flying through the air, skirts billowing, the partner of a Hollywood dancing star.

But Shirley was not to be persuaded otherwise, and I saw her off on the next Seattle bound boat. It saddened me greatly to see her go, but I knew her dreams were such that she had to try. She promised to keep me informed of her progress and whereabouts, but it occurred to me that if she was successful, it was unlikely I would hear from her in the future.

She waved as the barge pulled away from shore, and soon I no longer could distinguish her from other outbound passengers. An hour later the ship was merely a dot on the horizon, then soon gone.

For some weeks I did not hear from Shirley and I was deeply concerned, as I visualized her penniless and abandoned, standing forlorn on the corner of Hollywood and Vine. Much to my surprise and relief, I received a letter in early October written on the stationery of a major Los Angeles hotel. She had met and joined forces with a well-known producer who, she added with double underlining, said she had great possibilities as a dancer. I knew Shirley well enough to know she had exceptional talent, but not, I was sure, in the pursuit mentioned by the producer.

I did not directly hear from Shirley again. Two years later, I noted a familiar face on the poster advertising a new film at the Dream Theater. The movie was "Crazy Dancer" and the face was Shirley's. Only now she was called Mona Markham and she smiled toothily out at me.

Although I had not planned to spend time or money at the Dream Theater, temptation was too much. I paid my dollar and went inside, careful to take a seat, as instructed, on the right of the center aisle. At that time seats on the left were set aside for natives.

And there she was, unbelievably, my Shirley, whirling and stepping with a dark-haired partner, her flowing skirt swirling about her, just as she always had dreamed. It was wonderful and heart warming to see her there and to know the extent of her success. Mona Markham in time became a first rate star, and life, it seemed, had brought her the fulfillment of her fondest desires.

I left the theater dazed, but happy.

"Crazy Dancer," I whispered under my breath as I walked into the cool night air. "Who's crazy now?"

24

Mother Sawtooth knew and much admired Carlotta Sands. Carlotta was the widow of Mark Sands, one of Nome's most successful individual miners. Mark and Carlotta had come to Nome from southern California in the mid-thirties. Mark had made good money in heavy equipment sales, but the pressures of the huge metropolitan area began to perplex him. He knew Carlotta well enough to know that she, too, was ready for a change. They had been caught in an over-demanding social life, in much of which they had little interest.

Mark Sands was an adventurer, and particularly he

liked to hunt. Two safaris to Africa cured him of the desire to return to that continent, so he cast about for new hunting grounds to conquer. He always had wanted a polar bear trophy, so through a sportsmen's club in Los Angeles he contacted Manny Newton, who was guiding professionally out of Nome.

Manny flew his own small bush plane, ski-equipped for winter, as that was the only time of year polar bear hunting was feasible. The plane flew offshore over the sea ice until an animal was located. Then the real test of the pilot's ability came, for he had to land the plane safely on the uneven pack ice reasonably near the curious white bear.

Most of Manny's clients were heavy as well as wealthy, so a long and exhausting trek over the rough ice in cold winter weather was out of the question.

Once within range of a high-powered rifle, the bear usually was an easy shot, for the animals lived their lives on the arctic ice floes and had little knowledge or fear of man. Manny was a cocky little fellow and guaranteed clients a bear. "No bear, no pay" was his motto. However, Manny was careful always to back his hunter with his own well-aimed rifle in case the shot was a miss, or only wounded the hapless beast. Since the days of winter are short in the Arctic, the hunt usually took only three or four hours. Manny was careful to scout the area before his client arrived, so usually he knew generally the location of several animals.

Mark Sands arrived in Nome in February, and he had come the hard way. His route had been long and wearying, as he had traveled by rail to Seattle, by ship to Seward, by rail again to Fairbanks, and then westward to Nome in a small, open-cockpit Waco biplane piloted by Buster Wilkinson, one of Alaska's early-day bush flyers. Midway, when Buster lost his bearings for a short time and wandered aimlessly over the landscape searching for a particiular river junction, Mark cast his eyes skyward for as much aid as the Lord could provide. Apparently the call was heard, as the small plane, a few hours later, successully placed its skis on a snow covered hilltop just north of Nome.

From the beginning Mark was fascinated with Alaska, particularly the Nome area. The next day, Manny brought him to his bear, which he shot with much less enthusiasm than expected. The beautiful creature just reared to its hind legs and looked at him across fifty yards of glistening snow, its black nose moving back and forth in the wind to place the unknown scent of man.

Mark's shot pierced the silence and the unfortunate beast leaped frantically into the air, thrashing in a panic of pain and fright. It then lay still, and red blood colored the snow in a widening circle. The bear was a magnificent adult male in the prime of life, the pelt a beautiful thick white. Mark always kept his trophy, an unusual ten feet in length, but the manner of the animal's death bothered him so deeply that he never could bring himself to display the skin or brag to his friends that he had taken a polar bear.

Mark's stay at the Bonanza Hotel marked a turning point in the lives of Carlotta and himself. There he met and came to know Sam Green, who had mined the Nome area since 1906. Sam owned the Wolf Bar dredge and wanted to dispose of it. He never had done well at dredging. Placer mining was his forte. He liked personally to handle the gravel and wash the sluices, and the complex mechanism of the dredge appeared constantly at odds with him. Wolf Bar was good ground, the test drillings showed it, but Sam wanted out so he could reutrn to his Lucky Lady Creek claims in the Kougarok.

Mark was waiting for Buster to return to Nome in order to fly the same perilous return route to Fairbanks. Buster flew no schedules, nor did limited radio contact tell of his arrivals and departures. When he did come, Mark needed additional time to investigate further the possibilities of Wolf Bar dredge, as he had developed a serious interest. He telegraphed Carlotta that he was all right and would be home soon.

Mark talked Buster into flying him to Wolf Bar for a close, hard look at the dredge. Buster had no certain idea where Wolf Bar was located, but after an hour of flying they saw the dredge on the distant horizon at a sharp bend of the frozen Wolf River. Buster landed on a hillside nearby, where the snow had drifted deep enough to allow only the alder tips to show through. Mark was thrilled. It was a beautiful day, one of those arctic winter days in which the sun glistens brightly on every snow crystal, and the air felt deceptively warm.

Sam had given him the keys to the various doors and hatches, and a good flashlight, as all the windows of the dredge were boarded over for the idle winter months. Mark went over the machinery and hull so far as visible, with care. As Sam Green had warranted, all appeared to be in top condition.

Buster took off with an enthusiastic Mark in the cockpit before him. As he had flying over, in the now-ending day, for it was past three in the afternoon, Mark watched mile after mile of rolling marshmallow snow pass beneath the little plane and noticed the mountains in the distance, a lovely pink, the deepening color of the approaching arctic sunset.

The next morning the little Waco took off, skimming the trees and hilltops back to Fairbanks, a distance of over four hundred miles. In a briefcase, Mark had Sam's log sheets and all pertinent records related to the operation of the Wolf Bar dredge.

Mark knew what he wanted to do, but what of Carlotta? He wondered what her reaction would be when he told her he wanted to sell everything, buy a gold dredge and move to Nome, Alaska.

25

While in Nome, Mark had met Mother Sawtooth and she had specially honored him with an invitation to join us for supper. With the aid of her mysterious pantry, Mother had produced her customary gourmet repast, and Mark ate heartily of the cullard of northern peckbuck, smothered in garlic and other mild herbs. Since the season permitted unrestricted use of ice, the dessert was a frozen one, a bombe of winter walrus mulchun topped with sauce renobel. Coffee and good conversation followed in the living room, and when Mother's nodding head signaled the end of the evening, Mark graciously expressed his appreciation and departed.

This probably is a good opportunity to tell a little of Mother's pantry, for it held many mysteries. The small but well-stocked room was directly off the back cache of Sawtooth House, next to the downstairs honey bucket room and, if one came from the rear, strange odors filled the hall leading to the kitchen.

The pantry had been expertly and uniquely designed by Mother herself, with one shelf above the other. Row upon row of boxes, jars, marniwels, tins and regopots sat side-by-side, filling the shelves to overloaded, each carefully labeled and dated so Mother could tell the contents and distinguish the difference between them. The names of many have escaped me, but I specifically recall a large box of dried grono stems which she often used in bouillabaisses or soricines. Too, I remember jars and regopots of marinated carrots, broccoli and ogel greens. A special favorite of Mother's was elgenny root properly mixed with just the right amount of calister oil, and this elegant combination often found its way into many of her entrees and desserts. All these, and many others, Mother used on a daily basis in the preparations which ever surprised and delighted us.

But it is only right that I finish the story of Carlotta and Mark Sands. As is evident by now, I dislike leaving anything incomplete.

26

Carlotta Dickerson Sands was the daughter of Walter and Evelyn Dickerson. Walter was a world recognized economist at Blanchard University near San Diego. Aside from his teaching, he had written numerous well received books on his subject and was much sought after and consulted in all fields of economics. Thus, considerably more income than merely his salary as a professor came to the family through the years of Carlotta's childhood.

The family lived extremely well in a large home in Coronado and they were socially prominent in the area. Fate had been singularly kind to Carlotta Dickerson. She was the beautiful child of attentive parents who were careful not to spoil her. For this reason, her girlhood was more spartan than one would have surmised. But, in a careful way, she was denied nothing and she happily grew to young womanhood in the secure world her parents provided. At twenty-one, she was a lovely young woman of exceptional beauty—slender, of medium height, with ash-blonde hair, blue eyes and an infectious smile. She had graduated cum laude from Blanchard with a degree in home economics, which she thought she wanted to teach.

But teaching was not a reasonable expectation for Carlotta. She was much courted by many young men, all of whom she liked, but none of whom struck a serious chord in her heart.

Not long after leaving Blanchard, she met Millard Walsh, a well known publisher, who handled her father's writing affairs. Millard was twenty years Carlotta's senior, a bachelor, and he pursued her relentlessly. She was fascinated by his brash good looks, reputation, and obvious good fortune, and she agreed to marry him almost without forethought.

Her parents were heartsick, but helpless to change her mind once the commitment was made. Carlotta, as she later said, had made all her mistakes correctly, for the wedding was a society event, perfectly executed, and well noted in the press.

From the beginning the marriage was a calamity. Millard, a bachelor of forty-one at the time of this, his first marriage, was unable to face any of its responsibliities and he defensively accused Carlotta of accountability for his failures. Following a brief period of panic, Carlotta analyzed the situation and wisely reached the conclusion that the marriage could not last. She and Millard had lived as husband and wife less than five months, a period of time considerably less than it took to process and finalize the divorce. The year was 1922 and Carlotta had just passed her twenty-second birthday.

It was over five years before Carlotta accepted an invitation for a date, although frequent opportunities had been available to her. The disastrous marriage to Millard had made her wary and she was determined to make no such blunder again.

Shortly after the divorce she had been employed by an advertising agency, a new and fast-developing business. She enjoyed the work and the challenge to her originality and inventiveness. Women in this, or many fields of endeavor at that time, were unusual, so she had received a certain amount of attention simply because of her sex. Her "first" date was with an attractive young man who recently had established a law practice in the building in which she worked. As in the movie scripts, they met unceremoniously when the elevator, containing only the two of them, became immobile between floors. Although stranded for only a few minutes, the incident gave Dick the opening for which he had been looking. That evening, he waited for her at the entrance to the building and, when he shyly, but with a spark in his eye, asked her to dinner, her resolve softened and she could not say no.

Dick entranced Carlotta, but not in a romantic way. He was quick, witty, and full of bounce, but she wanted no more than his friendship. He was bright enough to recognize this and he did not pursue her.

But Dick became a lifelong friend, and it was through him that Carlotta met Mark Sands. Mark and Dick had been roommates in undergraduate school. Dick had gone into law, while Mark had braved the business world, with little success at first. After a time he had been employed by Crawford Heavy Equipment Co. as a buck salesman. Mark had the talent to evoke confidence when he met new people, and this ability served him well, as soon he began to earn substantial commissions. Carlotta met Mark, of all places, in the same elevator in which she had met Dick, when going to work one morning. Dick introduced them and she was fascinated with Mark's golden red hair, freckles, friendly dark eyes, and tall, slender frame.

Mark was certain he never before had seen a woman so beautiful and he was struck speechless, which was not his normal condition. However, as had Dick, Mark used the elevator meeting and his contact through his former roommate to come to know Carlotta well enough to ask her to join him at a company gathering. She accepted, but was careful not to appear over-anxious. From the beginning, Mark's presence had sent her pulse racing and brought a touch of moisture to her upper lip. Mark's natural ease and friendly and debonnaire good humor completely captivated her, and soon she saw his face staring at her from every photo ad that came across her desk, or found it floating through her mind at every moment of detachment. Mark's situation was little different, for Carlotta's voice, her face, her figure, were with him constantly.

One evening, not three months from the day they had

met, Mark suddenly took Carlotta's hands, drew her to him, and she responded with a passion of desire she did not know was within her. They were married the next week with only Dick as best man, Charlotte, Carlotta's close friend, as maid of honor, and Carlotta's parents present for the brief ceremony. Carlotta did not know she could love any man so well and so deeply. Mark became the center of her life and this devotion did not falter so long as she lived.

They had done well as a team. Mark had advanced with Crawford Heavy Equipment and, despite the depression, by the mid-thirties he was west coast manager of sales, with a move east to company headquarters to come in the near future. Carlotta, always slim and lovely in a totally unassuming way, was his partner in social business responsibilities. She loved their large, gracious home with its expanse of green lawn and trees. She entertained beautifully and with perfect ease. The Lord did not bless their union with children, but their adoration for each other was such that no problem was created by this omission.

Thus, when Mark arrived home from Nome with Sam Green's briefcase clutched well in hand, and an air of enthusiasm about him she had not seen for some time, she knew him well enough to sense that the world had changed for him while he had been away and that it was about to change for her.

Mark told her of Alaska, of Nome, of Wolf Bar dredge, of Sam Green, and of his desire to make a change, with such eagerness that no room was left for protest, not that she wanted to do so. It merely struck her as such a sudden and vast transition that a slower pace would have assisted her assimilation of its magnitude. But there was no time for ease of change, for already it was early March, and if they were to get in a full season of dredging, things would have to move fast.

Things did move fast. Mark wired Sam Green his acceptance of their negotiated price for the claims, dredge, equipment and all camp buildings. The California house was sold, belongings were stored, suitcases were packed and they were aboard a Seward bound ship by mid-April. Mark was in heaven and, because of Carlotta's deep love for him, which he amply returned, she was in heaven, too. He had resigned his position with Crawford, giving only two weeks notice, and his co-workers were astonished beyond recorded word when he announced his plans.

Carlotta was agog when she saw Alaska—its beauty, its vastness and its mystery. Buster Wilkinson met them at the depot in Fairbanks and hustled them through town to Weeks' Field, the small dirt airstrip, which was still usable, as Spring's sun had not yet sent it into a sea of melting snow. The little Waco was there, smelling as usual of gasoline and grease. They zoomed off into the bright April sky and Carlotta was so thrilled she hardly could contain her excitement. The hills, mountain ranges, valleys and still-frozen rivers rolled beneath them, showing early dark spots of the rushing thaw to come. When Nome's first gray dots appeared on the horizon, Mark pointed to their location for Carlotta. When he saw the expression on her face, he laughed and drew close to her ear. "Things could have been worse, you know," he shouted over the roar of the whirling propeller. "It could have been Africa!"

27

News had gone around Nome quickly that Mark Sands, the rich Californian, had purchased Wolf Bar dredge from Sam. Mother Sawtooth, of course, was one of the first to know, for she ever had an attentive ear to the grindstone for news of community happenings. She remembered Mark from his earlier evening visit, as she had been impressed by his good manners and breeding, something she claimed she rarely saw around the table at Sawtooth House.

When one thought of Prybar and his tattered shirts, Harvey, or Millwood, one felt some justification rode with Mother's complaint. But generally it was a happy group around the table, ready and anxious to partake of her gourmet preparations. I have said little of Mother's ability with mixer, whang and oven. She was an excellent baker, of course, and of all the breads, brokkens and cakes that came from her oven, we most enjoyed her crenacle muffins. These, she insisted, must be made with cold-storage eggs at least six months old in order to impart that certain sulphurous flavor we all so loved. Crenacle muffins, steamy and hot, dripping with eider grease and clofenberry jam, were gastronomic gluttonies never to be forgotten.

I mentioned cold-storage eggs. In the years before regular air transportation, food enough to last Nome through the long winter had to be delivered by the last boat. Thus, crates of eggs by the hundreds came for cold storage and, as the months went by, they became more and more tasty. Many an old-timer refused to eat fresh eggs, for they complained they had no flavor. With this analysis Mother agreed, and eggs less than six months old were not allowed in her kitchen.

Mother was partial to cakes and it was ever to her credit that always they were masterpieces of the baker's skill. Usually consisting of at least one layer, smothered in turquoise or green frosting and decorated with hoops and stringers, they were a sight to stagger sore eyes. Often people of the community prevailed upon Mother's good nature to ask her to make one of her specialty pastries for some important occasion such as a birthday or a divorce.

It should be evident by now that Mother Sawtooth toiled unsparingly of her strength to produce her edible masterpieces day after day. Except for Eureka, whose time and abilities were limited, Mother labored mostly alone. As time passed, we became concerned that the demands of her kitchen were too great. One evening after a dinner of exceptional poulardo stuffed with cotlik bongos and seasoned with sitran colavo, someone asked Mother why she did not bring more help into her kitchen. She considered the question, then responded with her usual astute and original reply.

"Too many cooks spoil the knitting," she said.

As in the past, we again were astounded by Mother's creative choice of words. She was, we concluded, a remarkable and unpredictable woman.

But I should conclude the story of Carlotta and Mark Sands. Theirs proved to be the story of the luck of the gold miner of which every prospector dreams.

28

Upon arriving in Nome, after surviving the original shock of what she saw, Carlotta bravely set to work to establish their home. She was fortunate to find, and to be able to buy, an old home at the west end of town with a spendid view of the sea and Sledge Island. The house was much in need of repair and remodeling and she set to work without hesitation to accomplish her goal. It was a rambling Victorian stucture with a round tower in front, which had been built at the height of the gold rush in 1906 by Jakie Melburg. Jakie had hit it rich on Frisco Creek and, before his money ran out, he managed to complete this, the house of his dreams. It had the charm of the period's fourteen-foot ceilings and enough "gingerbread" to satisfy the most particular of Victorian connoisseurs.

Since Mark totally was involved in preparations for the forthcoming dredging season and was deep in computations of orders for fuel oil, gasoline, tools, parts, food and other supplies, the full responsiblity for the house fell to Carlotta. Although many things remained to be finished, she basically completed her plans for the house by the time they left for Wolf Bar the first week of June. It obviously was going to be an early breakup and Mark did not want to miss his opportunity for a full season of dredging. He had hired his crew and camp helper early in May, and all were at the dredge camp awaiting Mark's arrival.

Carlotta was totally enthralled with life at camp. Wolf River was wide and easy flowing, with cold, crystal water quite suitable to drink. Dolly trout and grayling skittered about over the clean gravel and were easy to catch. Even a small run of salmon inhabited the river late in the season. She found the surrounding tundra beautiful in a new and strange way. Treeless, save for a few scrub willows and alders in the creek and river valleys, a profusion of wild flowers and arctic birds followed the receding snow line of every grass hummock and ridge. A small lake, some half a mile behind camp, was the home of ducks, geese, loons and an exquisite pair of whistling swans.

Carlotta discovered a small grassy knoll overlooking the lake, and from there she could see a lovely range of mountains in the distance. A large boulder placed by a considerate Nature furnished a perfect place to rest. It was here that she frequently came in the long summer evenings, simply to enjoy the beauty of the unspoiled countryside. Mark often came to her there, and they were able to join in the deep love they shared together and find a newer, even greater closeness between them.

Carlotta, however, was not idle. Mark had instructed her in the art of record keeping, both financial and inventory and, after a few dead ends and false starts, she handled this responsibility well. The days of spring and coming summer were endless light, for Wolf Bar was but a few miles below the arctic circle and the sun wheeled continuously about their heads.

Despite his dislike of the dredge, Sam Green had done an excellent job preparing the machinery for operation. High water of the spring runoff delayed the start for nearly ten days, but at last an impatient Mark started the motors one drizzly morning, the bucket line surged into action, and the season had begun. Mark was ecstatic. His happiness was so great he almost did not care whether the dredge produced the treasured gold or not. He secretly had worried about Carlotta's adjustment to Nome and Wolf Bar after her southern California life of comparative ease, but she obviously was happy and delighted to be where she was, and to do her part.

Though still learning, Mark was cautious and handled the dredge operation well. It was his strong suit, to work with and operate heavy machinery. After eight days of digging, he shut the dredge down for some minor repairs and adjustments and for the first cleanup. Every old prospector grubbing in the dirt of his meager claim should have been present to witness the result. The yield was beyond Mark's wildest dreams and far in excess of what he had been told was the maximum he could expect.

"You'll be lucky to break even, especially your first season," Sam Green had told him.

Others had been considerably less optimistic.

The riffle boards were a flowing mass of gold—nuggets, large and small—clogged and heaped in such profusion that Mark thought his good senses had left him. His pulse pounded in his head as he, with the help of Carlotta and Kevin, processed the cleanup. They were unprepared for this staggering result and when the gold trays they had brought from Nome were filled, empty mayonnaise and pickle jars were pressed into service.

Buster, who now mainly flew out of Nome, attended the camp's day-to-day needs as best he could with his small plane, landing on a gravel strip cleared two years earlier by Sam with his bulldozer.

Buster whistled long and low when he saw the trays and jars full of gold. Eagerly, in three trips, he transported the heavy, yellow metal to the bank in Nome. A week later, after retort and bricking, word came back from the bank in the form of a gold report sheet. At the then-price of slightly over twenty-two dollars an ounce, the cleanup had totaled just under two hundred thousand dollars. Mark and Carlotta were too stunned to react. They looked quizzically at the white, neatly typed account sheet, together with the bank's letter of inquiry as to what accounts Wolf Bar wanted to open with these funds, as if they had been written in Chinese.

Wolf Bar became the true bonanza story—the dream, the big strike legend of the time—that would be the subject of awed discussion in the mining world for years to come. Although some cleanups to follow were not as spectacular as the first, several through the next years exceeded it. Mark and Carlotta studied the results, as reflected in the bank accounts, with continuing disbelief.

The first weeks they were in Nome, Mark and Carlotta seriously had considered spending winters in California. However, when the first autumn came, they viewed such plans as foolish. They wanted to stay the winter in their newly renovated home. Carlotta continued to do a splendid job with the house and, by the following spring, it was as comfortable and elegant as Nome and its climate would permit.

Mark loved the old house with its pleasant view of the Bering Sea and they settled with ease for the winter. They became acquainted in the community and joined in social affairs, many of which they found unique and original. Particularly, they enjoyed the annual Roof Garden party, given in dead winter, at which everyone dressed in summer finery. Mark looked most handsome in his white duck trousers and pale yellow jacket and Carlotta, who had lost none of her stunning good looks, was lovely in a filmy summer dress. They also enjoyed the whist series, sponsored by Pioneer Igloo Number 1, to which many of the old sourdoughs came to play the game.

Mark and Carlotta had been in the North Country and had operated Wolf Bar for six years by the spring of 1941.

War was rumbling on the world's horizons, and it was rumored that critical supplies of fuel might be curtailed by the government for non-essential industries, including gold mining. Mark had planned to operate throughout the summer of 1941, but when requests came from Washington to conserve fuel he was disappointed, but patriotic enough to comply without complaint. The dredging operation had made them more than wealthy and he was willing to stand by until the crisis was over.

It was with wartime shutdown in mind that Buster flew Mark that spring to Wolf Bar. He went only to check the dredge, its moorings and hull after the winter, to see that all was safe for storage until operations could be resumed. Exactly what happened, no one ever knew. When the little plane did not appear that evening a search was organized by the few other flyers in the Nome area. The answer was not hard to find. Twenty minutes from Wolf Bar the wreckage of the little Waco was found, its fuselage half buried in a muskeg swamp. Mark and Buster had not survived.

The small community was shocked and grieved. Many came to Carlotta's aid, and without them she could not have continued. In the years that passed she traveled widely and found many interests, but Nome ever was home. She kept the house at the west end of town, to which she always returned, for she found in the solitude of its rooms a touch and a memory of the Mark she so dearly had loved.

29

It was Mother, of course, who led us from the doldrums of our sadness. She had come to know the Sands well, and her melancholy had affected us all. One day, several weeks after the accident, she suddenly appeared at the kitchen door, her old smiling self. She announced it was time we all overcame our grief and returned to normal, if nothing more, for Carlotta's sake. She needed bolstering and seeing so many long faces about town was not going to help her. So it was that the tragedy slowly slipped from our memories and Sawtooth House once again took on its familiar air of gourmet gaiety.

That evening, after supper, I asked Mother if she felt America would become involved in the conflict then raging in Europe. She paused a moment, then answered.

"Where there's fire there's smoke," she said.

I was astonished again at the depth of Mother's perception and the individuality of her phraseology. It seemed the perfect answer, timely and original.

In an effort to buoy our spirits, Mother had provided a superior repast. The dinner had begun with tarltons of lago broth with golar croutons. Then followed her widely acclaimed fresh elder leaf salad with mommy seed dressing. It was one of her greatest innovations. The main course was a bellor stew of kolus flank and new potatoes, covered with a lovely gravy seasoned with erasmus pod. We were agog with delight. Dessert followed—small kaylo tartlets frosted with melted crenna sugar and friddel.

When dinner was over, we adjourned to the living room where we enjoyed Mother's prucard of selamoder tea served with small, sugared locus cookies. It was a wonderful ending to an astounding culinary evening.

Mother was home in her kitchen, and all was well at Sawtooth House.

30

This seems an opportune time to tell as much of an ending as I know about Clover Blue Conzarro. Tony's death, and her flight from San Francisco, had brought her back to Nome at a time she least expected to return. But after a few days she found it good to be home again. In Nome she could find solitude when she most needed it, away from the carping voices of the world outside Alaska.

Clover Blue located, and occasionally saw, a few old friends from girlhood days, but mostly she found solace in being alone. Old Triple O had died some years earlier. She missed him greatly, his always steady and reliable advice, and the mildly caustic way, with a twinkle in his eye, he spoke to her. Of all her old Nome friends, his death left the largest void in her life.

A number of weeks after her return, Clover Blue received a telegram from a San Francisco address and from people she did not know. She was requested to return to San Francisco immediately. The mere thought of San Francisco terrified her. The cruel events leading to Tony's death were still too much a part of her. She simply could not go. She did not reply to the telegram. A second and more urgently worded wire was received two weeks later. She did not answer.

A few days later she was told that a chartered airplane had arrived in Nome from Anchorage, a man on board inquiring for her. The arrival of an airplane in Nome at that time was cause for comment, but the fact the person involved had come to find Clover Blue made the incident all the more interesting.

Later that day Clover Blue was not surprised to hear persistent knocking at her door. Glancing from a front window she saw a well-dressed middle-aged gentleman, brief case in hand. He was from the press or from the San Francisco district attorney's office, she was certain. She could face neither. The knocking continued. He was not to be discouraged. Clover Blue opened the door, observed him suspiciously, wishing for some way to get rid of him without being rude.

"Mrs. Conzarro?"

She nodded.

"My name is Melvin Becker," he said. "Sawyer, Belmont and Becker, lawyers of San Francisco. May I come in?"

A cold fall wind blew outside, forcing itself into the room. The now leafless willows near the entrance leaned and scratched against the house. Reluctantly, she opened the door further and stepped aside.

The attorney entered the small, simple room that served both as her living area and kitchen and walked directly toward a wooden table and chairs.

"May I be seated?"

"Yes."

"Mrs. Conzarro," he began. "Our firm represents..."

"I really find this very difficult," she interrupted. "It is so soon."

"I understand," he said, "but we had to find you. We are attorneys for..."

"Please, I can't. It's just too soon."

He looked at her, tears welling in her eyes, knew he had to make the break quickly.

"My dear lady," he said, rising to lean across the table toward her. "As far as we can determine, you are the sole heir of Tony Conzarro. You are a very wealthy woman."

Following Becker's visit, finances no longer were a problem for Clover Blue. She could live any place she wished to live, could buy or build any home she wanted in Nome or elsewhere. But now, more than ever, Nome again had become home, the place of her roots and her heritage, the place she found secure.

Several years passed before Clover Blue found the courage and heart to return to San Francisco. After a few days in the city, she walked to the area she considered to be her old neighborhood, although she really had lived there a very short time. She found the Golden Hotel had been demolished several years earlier. The China Cup was there, but the restaurant was closed and obviously had been for some time. The interior, as she peered through dingy front windows, was a shambles, long abandoned, chairs seat-down on the old tables. She smiled when she saw the "waitress wanted" sign still in the window, faded now and nearly unreadable.

A taxi took her to a corner near the building where Tony's beautiful apartment had been. The penthouse at the top retained its mysterious outward appearance, large picture windows looking to the Golden Gate and inner harbor. She wondered who lived there now and whether they had found happiness in so lovely a place.

The trip to San Francisco at this time was made necessary by the need to confer directly with Melvin Becker. Over the intervening years her business affairs had been handled by correspondence or by long-distance telephone. But now, major decisions for the future were required, as the income from the funds left her by Tony greatly exceeded her needs. It was her wish to establish a trust to assist deprived Alaskan children of any race to further their education.

She looked again at the penthouse windows. The memory still hurt, but she could cope with it now. On that dreadful day, a call from Chun Lin on their private line had told her that Tony was dead. As Tony had instructed her, and as she knew she must, she fled the apartment and San Francisco as soon as possible. Quickly she washed away all makeup, roughed her hair from the high styling of a recent visit of her hairdresser, and went ou᠆ the servants' back entrance.

What luck! A taxi at that moment rounded the corner,

and she was on her way. She barely had settled in the back seat, when the driver, speeding off, glanced at her in the rearview mirror.

"I just heard on the radio that old 'Hot Sheets' got it in Chinatown. Ka-boom! Right on the street."

Clover Blue could not answer. Traffic was heavy. Exhaust fumes began to nauseate her. One stop light, then another. It seemed endless.

"Hot Sheets' been around this town a long time. I saw him once, leaving the Fairmont. Good looking devil. You heard about him all the time, but you never saw much of him. Sure had a beautiful wife!"

The driver chuckled.

Then the station. Traffic tieup at the entrance. She dropped several bills on the front seat, bolted the cab. Hurriedly, she ducked into the building. She had to be on the next train to Seattle.

Clover Blue shuddered, then brought her thinking back to the present. She looked again at the apartment building across the street that had once been of such importance to her. "That life is over, all over," she told herself. "I've known that for a long time."

She turned to walk away, not looking back, not wanting to look back. And the sun shone bright and warm on her face.

31

Arne and Helga Olson were good friends of Mother's. They lived down the block on Third Avenue and Arne, particularly, was a help to Mother from time to time. He ran errands, got the mail from the post office, and occasionally helped in some of the heavier tasks around Sawtooth House. He appreciated fine things, although few of them had come to him in life, and he was careful of the items Mother particularly treasured. Some years before, Mother had purchased an antique Swedish bodelstand, together with its bowl, pitcher and twelve matching yanow cups. Arne especially loved this piece of furniture as it was similar to one in his own family home in Sweden.

By the early forties Arne no longer was a young man. In fact, he had stampeded ashore onto Nome's beach in 1900 with a folded tent, a shovel, and a canvas bag of used clothing. He was then twenty years old. Only two years before, he had left his native Sweden and his beloved Helga, to travel to America to establish a new life. His final promise to a tearful Helga was that, as soon as he had saved enough money, he would return to Sweden, marry her, and bring her to New York with him. New York had not been kind to Arne. He had arrived there after a long crossing and several terrifying days on Ellis Island, to find the city thronged with immigrants from nearly every European nation one could mention. He had little money left after three lean months of unsuccessful job hunting and, of all humiliating things, was forced to write Helga for funds. She responded quickly with all she had, no magnificent sum.

Arne knew he had to get out of New York before Helga's meager finances were exhausted. He could not ask for her help again, and he could see no job or future in that city. It was a major disillusionment to him, as he had quite seriously believed, as had so many others, the stories repeated in the Old Country, that New York's streets were paved with solid gold.

Upon his arrival in New York, Arne had received from a newly-met fellow Swede some advice that proved to be invaluable. Arne had heard that a large Swedish settlement existed in New York and he intended to locate it as the area in which he would live.

"No, no, don't go there," his friend advised in Swedish, the only language Arne then knew. "You've got to learn

English, and if you settle in Swedetown you never will. Make yourself learn English by living in another part of town."

The advice was of great value and it never would have occurred to Arne. He found a room, cold, foreign, and dismal though it was, in a wholly separate neighborhood from his countrymen, and settled there. Arne was not the product of advanced education, but he was not stupid. He amazed himself at how rapidly, in the face of necessity, he learned English, though he spoke with a strong Scandinavian accent that he never entirely lost.

Arne took the only work he could get, as a laborer with the Western Pacific Railroad. He knew the railroad job would get him out of New York and that his chances could be no less in the west than in the metropolis he was leaving. For nearly two weeks he rode westward in a boxcar with forty or so others who were escaping New York for the same reason. The trip was unorganized and dirty and the men were provided minimal food and water.

The workers were ordered out of the boxcar at Leland, Idaho, a rail junction at which Western Pacific maintained a rail gang barracks and cookhouse. But for events which developed at Leland, Arne could have found the encampment, with its dense, pine forest and clear, running river, to be enjoyable, as it reminded him of his native Sweden.

As all the boxcar men had learned to do during the long and springless ride across the nation, Arne had traveled without his pants. To ride otherwise invited quick and uncompromising wear to the seat as the car rattled and bounced along the tracks. The men were so advised by a two-time rider in their midst, and his advice proved sound. Since standing was nearly impossible as the boxcar rolled and swayed, all the men had to sit on the rough plank floor for most of the trip. Gaping holes in the seats of trousers would appear after only two or three days and, in the western railroad camps, new arrivals had come to be called "holey rollers" in deference to their exposed posteriors. Having been so forewarned, Arne and most of his fellow travelers rode pantless, sitting on a folded shirt or torn remnant of blanket. Even this padding wore into shreds as the days passed.

Not far from Leland, Arne had fallen into a fitful sleep dictated by sheer exhaustion. While thus vulnerable, some s.o.b. stole his pants. He was awakened to the call of his name, and the shouting of his traveling companions, that they had been ordered off the train at that stop. Already a number of others were on the ground lined up beside the car, which began to lurch forward. Frantically, Arne grabbed for his non-existant trousers, formerly folded neatly beside him. He could feel the car moving forward, faster now. In panic, he seized the few belongings left to him and bolted through the open boxcar door. Luckily, he kept his feet. Conscious of his unorthodox appearance, he looked for cover. There was none. Several men and some fifteen or twenty women and children, who had come from camp to see the train in and view the new arrivals, were staring in astonishment at his bare, hairy and pantless legs.

After several interminable minutes, the waiting foreman took pity on Arne's condition and gave him his jacket, which Arne gratefully utilized to cover himself. His audience, however, by that time had gone into screams of laughter. From that moment on, as long as he worked at Leland, Arne was known to all as "Bare Shanks" Olson. He hated it and vowed, for that reason alone, at the first opportunity, to move on.

His resolve to leave Leland was fortified one day when, on the camp boardwalk, he passed the wife of the railway junction supervisor. Arne was aware that she rarely ventured from her log home, and certainly she knew none of the laborers by name.

As she passed, she nodded briskly and, without a moment's hesitation, said, "Good evening, Bare Shanks."

Arne thought he detected a slight smirk, and blushed as he always did when a lady called him by that detested nickname.

The opportunity to move on came after Arne had been at Leland nearly three miserable months. Workers were wanted for a new trunkline near Bester, Oregon. Arne volunteered, packed his sparse possessions, and wrote a quick note to Helga that he was changing locations.

The trip to Bester was a relatively short one, taking only the better part of a day. Four others from Leland were transferred with Arne, three of whom were newly arrived from the east and not aware of Arne's hated epithet. The fourth, unfortunately, was Buck Parson, an old-timer at Leland who knew the "Bare Shanks" story well. Buck, also unfortunately, was a brute of a man who tended to be a bully. On the trip to Bester, Parson had called across the car to Arne, utilizing the hated name. Arne gritted his teeth and clenced his fists until his fingernails dug into the palms of his hands. He walked across to Buck and asked him to forget the "Bare Shanks" story, explaining that he was leaving Leland and wanted to leave that name behind, too. Parson only smiled and grunted.

Upon arrival at Bester, the five workmen descended from the car to be met by their new boss, Carlo Miller. Buck Parson, always forward and self-important, grasped Carlo in an over-familiar handshake, introduced himself, and turned to Arne.

"And this fellow," Buck said with more than a touch of sarcasm, "is 'Bare Shanks' Olson."

"Who?" queried a puzzled Carlo.

Arne reddened.

"This here's 'Bare Shanks' Olson," Buck repeated with mock concern. "Tell him, 'Bare Shanks', how you got your name."

Arne was a peaceful man, but anger rose within him with such velocity, and to such a peak, that he hardly realized what was happening. He had been humiliated and taunted too long because of the despised "Bare Shanks," and he was determined the name should not follow him any longer.

With the quickness of a snake at a gopher, Arne swung at Buck with all the pent-up strength his anger had induced and caught his tormentor squarely under the left side of his chin. Buck flew into the air spinning and spiraling vertically like a child's top, and came down in a heap, spewing blood and teeth over the gravel roadbed. He gurgled, sighed, then passed out.

Carlo Miller, a rotund little man who peered at the world through round, steel-rimmed spectacles, momentarily was speechless. All, including a bewildred Arne, looked down at Buck Parson as he lay ignominiously in the dirt, his head propped askew against a stack of newly-tarred railroad ties.

"I don't want this kind of trouble here," stated Carlo, "and sure as Hell is fire, when this man wakes up there's going to be trouble."

He motioned Arne back onto the still motionless railcar. "You go on to Willow Junction," Carlo said. "Tell Elder I sent you 'cause I had too many men. Not too far wrong, either," he chuckled, nudging a still-sleeping Buck with his foot, "'cause when this bruiser comes to, one too many, Sonny, is what there's gonna be if you're still here." Gratefully, Arne hopped aboard the now-moving car. As he looked back, he saw Buck's fingers slowly clenching and unclenching. Arne knew his short stay at Bester nearly had been too long.

At Willow Junction, Elder received Arne with a cold look and a shrug of his fat, soft shoulder.

"Carlo is sending too many men along," he stated. "Pretty soon we're going to have enough around here to build this railroad to the moon."

Elder surveyed Arne suspiciously.

"How'd you hurt your hand?" he asked.

In surprise, Arne looked for the first time at his puffy, cherry-red right hand. The fingers were stiffened and swollen like pieces of iron pipe.

Before he could answer, Elder said, "You better go on into the main terminal at Seattle. Tell 'em Elder and Carlo sent you 'cause you're real handy with your dukes." Elder chuckled at his own humor, his gross belly shaking like custard in a pot.

Two days later Arne arrived in Seattle, a small town pushing up the slopes of two or three hillsides. He left the railroad there, as the thought of Buck Parson rounding a boxcar and lunging at him, had haunted him since that day in Bester.

32

It was nearly five years before Arne returned to Sweden. Of course the circumstances which brought him to Seattle in the fall of 1899 were wholly fortuitous. He had left New York with the plan to work for the railroad as long as necessary to save enough to return to his waiting Helga. Although he was not saving money at a rapid rate, if it had not been for the grievous "Bare Shanks" affair, he could have stayed in Leland and, in two or three years, saved enough to accomplish his marital goal.

Arne got a job rooting stumps from Seattle's muddy Pike Street. Several men on the work gang had followed the gold seekers through Skagway, Dyea and over the Chilkoot Pass to the Klondike. All in the group had returned penniless and disappointed, but in no way discouraged by the severe hardship several had endured. The gold fever bug had bitten these men severely, and no medication to counter its effects seemed to have been developed. Gold, in fact, was the major subject of conversation among the workers. Arne heard stories of fortunate miners with their cans and pokes of nuggets, and the riches a few had found by perseverance and luck. He had not forgotten his disappointment in New York and his curiosity was aroused by what he had heard.

Rumors of a big strike on Alaska's Seward Peninsula had been circulating for several months. Communication was lacking, however, and nothing could be confirmed. The few ships that traveled that way had not bothered to stop in the general region of the rumored activity, so very little that could be substantiated was known.

The dam broke in the May of 1900. The Anvil Creek strike was verified, as were impressive gold finds along a stretch of beach on the south shore of the Seward Peninsula. In haste, ships were provisioned and space sold for passage to the Anvil Creek area. Hundreds, then many hundreds, of gold-hungry men tried to book passage. The ships available could not handle the need, and those that sailed from Seattle were overloaded.

Arne reported for work the morning after the big Alaska gold strike had been announced. Of a work force of twenty-eight men, only Arne and three others appeared. The stampede to Anvil Creek and gold-rich beaches nearby was on, and Arne determined to become a part of it.

Arne's presence in Seattle at that time was a stroke of luck as it enabled him to book passage on one of the first northbound ships to sail. He had purchased a small tent, some used warm clothing, and a shovel. He knew no more than that concerning the needs of his destination or his newly chosen career.

The *North Star* sailed from Seattle on a bleak and rainy June morning with nearly four hundred men on board. Even open deck space sufficient to allow a man to lie down was at a premium, so Arne found it difficult to locate comfort for his lanky frame. Meals were served by a galley staff not trained to the volume of the task, nor was the dining space sufficient to serve so many men. It was a miserable eighteen days as the small and overloaded ship plied the Gulf of Alaska and the Bering Sea to Anvil Creek.

Arne's first glimpse of the shore revealed numerous tents of all sizes and shapes crowded upon the beach. Men were working everywhere, bringing sand to the long sluice boxes and then washing it down with water usually carried in buckets by hand. There appeared to be no organization to the manner in which the tents were pitched or to the beach area worked, and indeed there was none. Each tent owner worked the land which his tent covered and as much of the surrounding area as he could, competing with his neighbor for nearly every shovelful of sand or gravel to go into the sluice box.

Quarrels, fights and bitter disputes were commonplace and often firearms appeared and were used. Life was cheap and death came easily. No law, or semblance of law, existed. The big, the strong and the forceful prevailed. It was into this world that Arne stepped, carrying his tent, his bag of clothes, and his shovel.

In times to come, Arne had difficulty recalling the events of those first three years of turmoil and chaos on the beach, followed by mucking the claims on Goldengate Creek. This was the area which soon came to be known as Anvil City and, finally, Nome. For an inexperienced miner, Arne did well, but prices were so high for basic necessities that he could put aside only a small percentage of his take.

Anvil City had grown across the beach and back a few hundred feet onto the tundra with surprising speed. By the end of Arne's first summer, saloons, restaurants, grocery and hardware stores and banks had been established in clapboard buildings erected by their owners in record time, to reap the harvest of the miners' needs. The winters were idle, cold and difficult, but most of the men persevered, visions of shiny gold and fortunes to be made constantly with them.

In 1904 Arne sold his best claim on Goldengate Creek for thirteen hundred dollars, took his small savings and sailed for Seattle on the last boat of the season. He was on his way to retrieve his beloved Helga. Mail to and from Anvil City at best was sporadic and Arne and Helga had not heard from each other for some time.

Upon arrival in Seattle, Arne quickly wrote Helga a note that he was on his way, somehow assuming that the letter would arrive in Sweden before he did. He boarded a train for Chicago, then New York. He sailed for Amsterdam as soon as ship's passage could be arranged, and three weeks later he was running down the village street to Helga's parents' home. He expected her to be watching for him, running to meet him, her light brown hair flying behind her in the wind. The whole scene had been rehearsed in his mind, but she did not meet him.

Helga, who of course had not received Arne's letter, and more and more had come to visualize herself as a forlorn spinster, was in the barn unromantically milking the goats before supper. Arne found her there, so startling the poor and lonely girl that her screams stampeded the skitterish goats through the door, overturning several pails of milk. It was a tearful and joyous reunion and they were married the following week.

Arne told Helga of Alaska, of Anvil City, of the gold claims he still owned there, and of his desire to return. For Helga's part, she had no intention now of allowing Arne to go across the village without her, much less to the end of the earth, and she considered Alaska just that. So, with goodbyes to parents and lifelong friends, the newlyweds embarked for New York and then for Alaska.

Arne and Helga returned to Anvil City to find his remaining claims on Goldengate Creek jumped and worked by others. Although he tried, he was unable to oust the imposters or gain recompense for his loss.

They settled into the community and, thereafter through the years, Arne worked for others. But, for a very secret reason he did not confide even to Helga, he loved the isolation of Nome, as the town soon came to be called. The reason was simple. He was far away from Leland, Idaho and Buck Parson, so no one ever again called him "Bare Shanks."

33

The Fourth of July was always a gala occasion at Mother Sawtooth's. Of all her noble qualities, patriotism was one of the most leading. Sawtooth House was a blaze of color, with white, red and blue fandangos everywhere. Eureka and Mother spent many hours to make the house the most brilliantly decorated in the community. It was a sight of retinal splendor. Flags waved from all the second story porte cocheres, and cloth streamers were aglow with color and luminosity.

For this particular day, Mother had acquired a beautiful, blooming plastic azalia. It rested in a prominent place on the mahogany rickoshay in the front hall. Mother explained that she much preferred artificial plants as they were so easy to keep alive, and for this reason she liked them better than dead, live ones.

Each year on Independence Day, we all looked forward eagerly and with renewed anticipation to see Mother's widely acclaimed Fourth of July apron. Over the years, she had labored with her own light-fingered hands to produce this fascinating piece of stitchery. The deep blue blouson top was marked in even rows of forty-eight white stars, two of which were extra large and strategically placed. The skirt billowed in diagonal stripes of red and white, and the entire garment was tied in back with an enormous bow of blue and red crepe de chine which had been lined with rickrack to ensure that it kept its shape and fortitude.

And who could but rest in awe and amazement at Mother's traditional Fourth of July dinner. It was served with great fanfare of exploding firecrackers, with Eureka dancing about the table, sparklers aglow in each hand. The meal began with Mother's famous Independence Soup, a secret mixture of beluga puree and mossberries, which gave the liquid a sparkling blue color. Star-shaped noodles were a panacea afloat on the surface. We were entranced. Then followed the George Washington salad, a mixture of fresh, green Mt. Vernon nogales dressed in red sacona and oil dressing. The salad was a favorite of all who were fortunate enough to partake of its delectables and, for many, it was the piece de restrainment of the entire meal. But, with Mother in the kitchen, such decisions were difficult, for the traditional main course quickly followed.

Mother entered the dining room as Millwood and I set off additional firecrackers and skyrockets, carrying her astonishing constitution of ukeros, smothered in broiled kestellian puffballs and corgon relettos. Around the edge of the large forchette upon which this remarkable concoction was served, were mangles stuffed with mahjonggs and phefferness. We were aglow with delight. Millwood served with his usual awkward aplomb.

The dessert was Mother's cones de Valley Forge, a frozen combination of iced davits arranged in red, white and blue stripes and covered with flaming Ben Franklin sauce. Truly, the Fourth of July at Mother's was a gastronomic accosting long to be remembered.

34

For some time we noted that Prybar frequently had gone out in the evenings, a habit entirely new to him. Word soon filtered back to Mother that he was wonder-eyed at the new billing clerk at Norwell's Clothing Emporium. Rebecca was no blushing child, as it was evident she never would pass forty again. But then, Prybar was no longer of tender years, either. We noticed too, that Prybar's shirts suddenly had acquired buttons and that new suspenders protected his pants from the forces of gravity. One evening, without notice, he brought Rebecca to dinner. She was a pleasant woman, a bit awed by Mother's splendors, and not prone to excessive conversation, as she said hardly a word the entire evening. Fate had endowed her with a spindly figure, broomstick legs, and a considerably more than ample nose, but Prybar looked upon her with misted vision.

Nervous in the presence of so great a personage as Mother Sawtooth, Rebecca managed to spill her coffee and to cause a piece of Mother's patrie cake with escargot frosting to descend to the dining room carpet. All in all, it was not the best evening for Rebecca, but Prybar was blissfully unaware of it all.

When Prybar left with Rebecca to walk her home, Harvey asked Mother if she thought the affair was serious. Mother reflected for a moment and replied, "All's well that ends well."

Again, the best of all possible answers—original and to the point.

One evening several weeks later, Prybar had called for Rebecca as usual, at closing time, at the front entrance to Norwell's. It was no secret that Rebecca had become seriously enamoured of Prybar. But, for her, it became an evening of unhappy memories.

Rebecca always had been careful to look more or less directly at Prybar, never allowing her profile to be too much in evidence. That night the mist cleared from Prybar's eyes when, unknown to her, he got a good solid look at her features silhouetted against the lights of the store. He was shocked upon noting for the first time the true proportions of her protruding nose, and to realize how very much she resembled his former wife, Sylvia. Strange, he never had noticed that before. Suddenly, her speech and every mannerism of the unfortunate woman became Sylvia all over again.

The romance cooled and Prybar, buttons now loose and new suspenders showing signs of wear, retreated to the safety of Sawtooth House.

It was about this time that Mother received another letter from Kirk. Several months had passed since his last letter and, although we had discussed the matter in her absence, we had reached the conclusion that, in all probability, she never would hear from him again.

The arrival of the airmail envelope, addressed in Kirk's carefully slanted script, had a strange effect upon Mother. She read the letter several times, brow furrowed, and then, as usual, tucked it carefully into the safety of her bosom.

It was at this time too, that I again suggested to Mother that she record her wonderful and unusual gourmet recipes. She nodded her head as if in assent, as she had the last time, so I was enouraged to think that soon the kitchen masterpieces of Nome's Mother Sawtooth safely would be recorded on paper.

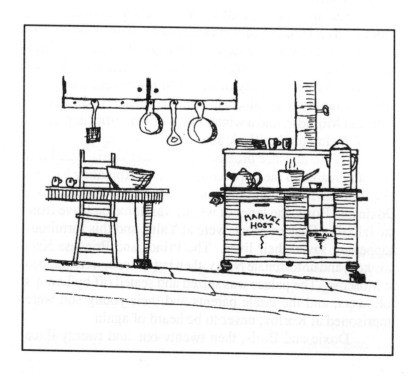

35

The Northern Adventurers' Club was located on Bourbon Creek just off Bessie Road, about one-half mile north of the Nome city limits. It was a large building, a remodeled early-day airplane hangar located on the edge of the now-overgrown gravel stretch of Nome's first airstrip. The exterior belied the interior, for the former was paint-worn and shabby, but the latter was inviting, tasteful, and well furnished.

The club was operated by long-time Nome resident Doxie Howard, a trim, majestic blonde whose appearance failed to suggest her nearly fifty years. It is difficult to tell the story of Doxie.

She was Russian, of the Karbosikov family, long a prominent and noble banking family of Imperial Russia. The family's ancestry was traced to the days of Peter the Great who, in the early seventeenth century, relied on the Karbosikovs to finance many of his royal reform programs. In 1917 the family maintained sumptuous palaces in St. Petersburg and Moscow, and a winter home of magnificent proportions at Yalta, on the Black Sea.

Doxie and her brothers, Nicky and Boris, had been born and reared in the imperial splendor of Romanov Russia. The Bolshevik Revolution caught the family by surprise. Doxie and Boris, the latter of whom was home on leave from the faltering Eastern Front, were at Yalta, and this fortuitous happening saved their lives. The Prince and Princess Karbosikov, and unfortunate Nicky, then but sixteen, were trapped in Moscow. The palace was seized and sealed off by Lenin's followers, and the noble parents and their young son were imprisoned at Korlov, never to be heard of again.

Doxie and Boris, then twenty-one and twenty-three

respectively, had limited time to organize their escape. A major part of the exquisite family jewels, by chance in the vaults of their Yalta winter home, were all the two reasonably could salvage before the holocaust of the Revolution reached Yalta. These, Doxie and Boris packed into a small valise and, in ill-fitting clothing, they began a long trek to the east, for they had been warned that it was impossible to cross to the west. The valise contained a staggering fortune, the Karbosikov jewels.

The trip eastward across Asia was a nightmare of cattle cars on the Trans-Siberian Railroad, delays, periods of hiding, and long, exhausting walks between stations and villages, as frequently the residents were at odds with one another. In future years, Doxie found it impossible to recall in detail all the perilous escapes and frightening confrontations of her travels with her brother.

Arrival at Vladivostok, months later, found them exhausted and lacking funds for the basic requirements of life. Boris, forced to set aside the risks of discovery, decided to take a lesser ruby and diamond brooch that had belonged to their grandmother, to a local money dealer to exchange for cash. The dealer eyed him suspiciously, wondering aloud how a person of Boris' shabby appearance could possess such a valuable piece. To hurry the transaction, Boris accepted far less than the brooch was worth, even on the money lenders' market.

He hurried to find Doxie, who nervously was waiting for him with the valise near the entry to a small inn. They booked an uncomfortable and drafty room for the night and, in order not to raise suspicion, registered as husband and wife.

The following morning Boris felt uneasy, that they probably were being watched, and decided it was imperative they leave as soon as possible. Their ultimate goal was far to the north: East Cape, Siberia. Many weeks time and a long series of small coastal trading and fishing vessels took them north from settlement to settlement. Always, the precious and battered valise somehow was saved and, more than two years after fleeing Yalta, following long and punishing months, they arrived at East Cape from which they could see across the cold sea to Alaska. Gone was the ease of the privileged nobility. Doxie and Boris, long before then, looked the parts they originally had attempted to play. She, gaunt in a tattered coat pulled close around her in the October arctic wind and he, the sophisticated Boris of St. Petersburg and Moscow society, dark-bearded and drawn from the effects of deprivation and cold.

Across fifty miles of the Bering Straits lay Alaska, formerly Russian America, and Alaska's dim and misty shore spelled safety and release to them. With the aid of a magnificent emerald ring that had been their mother's, they convinced a native hunter he safely could land them at Cape Prince of Wales on the Alaskan mainland.

The craft was a small umiak, an open boat made of walrus skin stretched on a driftwood frame. The motor, a worn outboard of Russian make with the flywheel side-mounted, pushed the frail craft bearing Doxie, Boris and their valise across an angry sea. Great waves battered the small boat, which was no more than fifteen feet long, and it seemed at times the Alaskan shore was receding from their view.

The perilous crossing became another ordeal in the long history of their flight. The frigid October wind blew at nearly gale force when they reached the straits. The Diomede Islands were on their left as they passed the international date line and into American territory. Boris, numb and stiff with cold, fought the motor handle from the native navigator who, in a panic of fright in the frothy sea, attempted to turn back to the Siberian coast.

Sixteen hours after embarking from East Cape, the frail craft neared the Alaskan shore. Enormous breakers thundered toward the beach, fell in great foaming masses of dark and icy water, surged over the sand, and receded, in a turmoil of raging sea. The little umiak drew near the shore, but could not land.

"Jump, Doxie, jump!" Boris shouted, for it was their only chance. Clutching the precious valise, Boris threw himself into the rushing surf. Doxie, in a daze of cold and fear, followed him. Somehow, some way, she made it to shore, soaked and iced to the bone. Boris did not follow her. He was gone, and she never saw him or the valise again. The wind hit like a knife as she pulled herself from the sea. She looked at the buffeted and blowing grasses of the Alaska beachhead and sank to her knees. Then, mercifully, all consciousness was lost to her and she fell onto the cold, wet sand.

The small Eskimo village of Wales sits at the Western tip of the Seward Peninsula, and it was young Timothy Menapuk, in search of driftwood on the beach, who found Doxie. At first he thought some bundle or crate from a ship at sea had washed ashore, as such a happening occasionally occurred. As he drew near he saw it was the body of a young white woman, but he thought she was dead.

Timothy ran to his mother's small, earthen-topped home. Fannie Menapuk for a moment would not believe her son's story, but when she realized he was serious she donned her parka, seized a large reindeer skin coverlet from the communal bed, and quickly followed Tim to the beach.

October is a stormy and difficult month at Cape Prince of Wales. For the most part, fall has given way to winter and snow already has drifted into the hollows. A cold wind from the west or southwest pressures the land incessantly, as if to push it back to some invisible line beyond which it should not encroach. The sky looms bleak and gray as cloudbank after cloudbank races to the north and east. The tundra grass lies flat to the ground and all life has retreated from view. Tim led Fannie to the soaked and frigid mound on the beach. Fannie knew the north country and the laws by which life endures, and she knew there was no time to lose. Quickly, with experienced hands, she stripped the wet and freezing clothes from Doxie's body and, with one rolling motion, she spun her into the fur side of the dry reindeer skin. With Tim's aid, the bundle was lifted to her shoulder, and Fannie struggled over the uneven ground to the small, but reasonably warm home.

Carefully she laid her burden on the bed.

"Get snow, Tim, a bucket of snow."

The boy darted outdoors and soon returned with an ample supply of the one commodity not scarce to the arctic. Fannie rubbed Doxie's feet with snow, then her hands, her ears, and her nose. Slowly, as the night progressed, warmth began to return to her body.

It was three days before Doxie regained consciousness. Fannie was frantic that she would not come to her senses in time to eat, for the body was pitifully thin and she knew death from starvation and thirst was a pressing possibility.

When finally Doxie stirred, Fannie was ready. Deftly, she spooned warm meat broth into Doxie's mouth, saying only, "Swallow it, swallow it. You have to eat."

Doxie did not understand the language, but she sensed the urgency of the words and she obeyed.

When spring came, Doxie had been with Fannie for nearly eight months and strength had returned to her body. The insistent sun of June had melted the snow and life was returning to the north. Doxie watched fascinated as sea birds by the thousands flew past to the rookeries on Farway Rock and the Diomedes. Wild flowers pushed through the greening tundra grass and bloomed in a profusion of color. From her meager supplies, Fannie had sewn Doxie two dresses, stockings, fur mukluks for her feet, and a parka. Fannie laughed and called her, "my Eskimo girl."

Fannie was a practical woman. She had been educated at the Jesuit mission school at St. Mary's Igloo, a small settlement not far from Nome. She had completed six grades, which was far beyond the norm for her time. At fifteen, she married Silas Menapuk, the lad from the village of Wales intended for her. Timothy was born two years later, but that same year Silas had not returned from hunting seal on the sea ice, and she was left alone. Fannie worked each day cleaning the newly constructed Native Service school, and by this means she had provided a scanty living for herself and her son.

The loss of Boris was a tragedy so acute in Doxie's life that she never could discuss it with others. The memory of his drawn, thin face and hollow eyes as he turned to her before plunging into the surf, were to go with her to her grave. She knew she could not indefinitely stay with Fannie, and that some plan for her future had to be developed.

Fannie, it turned out, was a natural teacher and by the time spring came, Doxie was making herself understood in English, mixed occasionally, much to Fannie's amusement, with a smattering of Eskimo.

Through the Native Service teachers at Wales, Doxie learned that a U. S. Customs port of entry existed at Nome, and she resolved to travel the one hundred twenty-five miles east to that city to report her presence in the United States, the manner of her arrival, and to request asylum. It was a tearful farewell that saw her into an umiak of native people bound for Nome. Fannie, that strong and good woman, tears streaming down her plump cheeks, stood on the beach waving a large white cloth for as long as the umiak was in view. Doxie could only look back once to return her salute, as her eyes were too clouded to allow her to see.

Although she was well-clothed and warm in the parka Fannie had made for her, Doxie's presence again in an open umiak chilled her, as the frightful trip from Siberia was still very much with her. After twelve hours the craft was pulled onto the beach west of the Nome sandspit, Doxie said goodbyes to her friends from Wales village, and walked to the center of town. It was late June of 1920.

The incredible story of Doxie's trip across Siberia

with Boris, their long trek to East Cape, and the umiak trip across the straits to Cape Prince of Wales, was heard by an astonished Customs agent. She was permitted to stay with an alien visa and, when qualified several years later, she became a United States citizen in the quaint old courtroom of the Territorial District Court at Nome. Although it had not been her original plan, she stayed in Nome the remainder of her life, as the little town became a refuge for her, a place far removed from the memories of Moscow, St. Petersburg and Yalta.

At first, Doxie worked at any job she could get. But as time passed she made close friends in the community and entered business, first with a small restaurant she called "Fannie's," in honor of her good friend, and then toward the late thirties she acquired the abandoned North Star Airlines hangar at the city field just north of Nome. It took time, but after a year's hard work she was able to open the Northern Adventurers' Club, a combination restaurant, cocktail lounge and night club. It proved to be a great success and was the realization of a dream for her, to have a place of her own, well-run and popular in the community.

Two years after her arrival in Nome, Doxie had married Wilbur Howard, a tug boat captain and coastal trader. The marriage did not last, but they separated friends. She kept his name, however, and always thereafter was known as Doxie Howard.

36

For a number of years during the early forties, Parnell Smith had played the piano for dancing and pleasant listening at Doxie's Northern Adventurers' Club. He had drifted to Nome as so many had, to work the mines, but after a few seasons, when he received a good offer from Doxie to return to his first career, he became her piano man.

Parnell was one of those naturally gifted musicians from whose fingers flow melody and rhythm, perfectly matched. He loved to play, he played extremely well, and he could play anything. For long hours each evening he sat at Doxie's grand piano and sweet music like few had heard before poured from his hands. Before long he was known simply as "sweet piano man," and indeed he was just that. His blues, his ballads, his Dixieland, even the classics, all were stored within his musical soul, and he was happiest when relaxing at the keyboard, almost into a dream, as melody issued forth.

The war came in 1941 and it changed Nome. Marks Air Force Base was well under construction just west of town by 1943, but its cross runways had been usable, though not completed, since the summer of 1942. Hundreds of military aircraft were ferried from bases in the lower states, through Canada, to Fairbanks, Nome, then Siberia, and finally to the Soviets' hard-pressed Eastern Front. American pilots flew the bombers and fighters as far as Fairbanks or Nome, where red stars were affixed in place of white, and Soviet pilots took the controls. Each day, and often through the night, formation after formation of these planes flew into Nome, peeled off, and landed for refueling.

For the purpose of handling the transfer of aircraft, the Soviet government maintained a contingent of airmen and supporting personnel at Nome. Their commanding officer was Colonel Gregor Yechenko. He once had been a handsome man, but at forty-nine, the Revolution, the years of struggle to build the Soviet Union, and now the war, had taken their toll. As commander of the small and isolated Nome garrison, he felt shunted aside and forgotten.

The Soviet contingent kept mostly to itself, and rarely did the men or their Colonel leave the barracks provided for them at Marks Air Force Base. For most, it was a transient life—west across Alaska from Fairbanks to Nome, and then across to bases in Siberia, where other waiting pilots took the controls to continue the long flight to the war's Eastern Front. From those Siberian bases, the men were ferried back to Alaska in groups aboard transport planes, to begin the tiresome flight over again in other aircraft.

Only a few in the community succeeded in getting Colonel Yechenko to join a dinner party or other social event. Most successful was Maynard Willard who often invited the Colonel to one of the lavish entertainments he frequently hosted at his apartment. Often, but not always, the Colonel came. He spoke English well, and was an excellent and interesting guest. When she was in town, Maynard always included Carlotta Sands among those on his guest list and nearly as often, Doxie Howard.

It was at such an evening at Maynard's that Doxie met Colonel Gregor Yechenko. Although she never was to recall the occasion as other than their first meeting, it was not the first time they had met. In the beginning Doxie was wary of him, as she, of course, knew who he was, and that he served as commanding officer of the Soviet airmen at Nome. As time passed, however, a certain bond of cautious friendship developed between them, and one evening as they were leaving Maynard's, she extended an invitation to him to visit her Northern Adventurers' Club. Politely, and with a slight bow, he declined.

But in spite of every effort at diversion, Colonel Yechenko could not get Doxie Karbosikov from his mind. He realized she did not recognize him, but in all fairness, after over twenty-five years, it was understandable that she should not. The desire to see her overcame him, and toward late evening four days after Doxie's invitation, he invented an excuse to leave the barracks alone and headed his Jeep toward the Northern Adventurers' Club.

Sweet piano man was playing when he entered, and the joy of hearing the music filled Gregor with a strange happiness he had not felt for years. It had been a slow evening and Doxie was preparing to close for the night. She had sent her kitchen and dining room help home and was resetting the last of the tables before leaving. He caught her off-guard as he stood looking across the expanse of polished dance floor.

"Good evening, my Colonel," she said in their native Russian. "You are welcome, but as you see, I am ready to close."

"I understand, my lady," he replied, also in their native tongue, and began to move toward the door.

But then, before Doxie could speak, instructed by that inner sense talented musicians seem always to have, to play the right melody at the right moment, sweet piano man, at first most softly, began to play the haunting and beautiful songs of Old Russia. The music grew in volume and pervaded the room with sweet sadness and ever increasing rhythms. The melodies filled the souls of Doxie and Gregor with memories, so long repressed, that they burst upon the two facing each other with irresistible strength. He stepped forward and she to him, and the music long gone from their hearts carried them about the dance floor in overpowering joy. As she had done as a maturing young woman at her parents' palace in Moscow, she danced with her partner in total abandonment. She saw again the red-carpeted grand staircase and her elegantly dressed mother and father descending to greet their guests at the Christmas Ball, the huge, shimmering crystal chandeliers, and the beautifully dressed men and women whirling to the music of violins and balalikas. She saw again her brother Boris, charming and friendly, and the officers of her father's guard, handsome in the formality of their uniforms. As the music played she heard again her mother's voice cautioning her, as she always had, not to be too forward, and she felt again the excitement and joy of those years, so short a time and now so long ago.

Gregor, every ounce of his Soviet military training impelling him to the contrary, remembered, too. The music, so long unheard, carried him aloft to the days of his youth, when as a young guardsman at the Karbosikov Palace, he had watched from across the room while a sophisticated and youthful Doxie danced with the guests at her parents' Christmas Ball. He remembered her, mature and lovely for her years, beautifully gowned, in the arms of a partner, swirl to the music of the orchestra, her happy laugh reaching him at the far side of the room. No longer, he knew, could he allow himself the luxury of recalling those faraway days, but sweet piano man, aware of the world they were for so short a time recapturing, played on until, at last, they stopped, drew back, and looked at one another. It was not Doxie, but Gregor who was weeping. Quickly, he took her hand, then released it. "Good night," he said, and walked briskly toward the door. He stopped, turned, looked at her searchingly for a few short moments.

"Good night, my lady," he stated softly, almost inaudibly, but she heard his words. Then he was gone.

Shortly thereafter, at his own request Gregor was reassigned to one of the bases in Siberia. Doxie never saw him again, but sweet piano man, the music, and that hour with him ever were in her heart.

37

Norton Sound green radishes were considered quite a delicacy and luxury by most Nomeites. Mother Sawtooth, of course, had created several recipes for their gourmet use. Who would have assumed otherwise? She had worked over the years with the pesky green things, for they were not easy with which to cope, to develop a splendid relish mixed with moddel seeds, to break a bit of the testy flavor.

Norton Sound green radishes grow only in the Nome area and once Mother had broken the ground, so to speak, to utilize their uniqueness, others began to follow suit. Many tried to imitate her fabulous relish, and others analyzed and attempted to copy, but with little success, her green radish souffle or her rizzola of green radish with Iona buckberry sauce and pikorie.

It was difficult to gather Norton Sound green radishes. They seldom were common over the local tundra, and it required both patience and fortitude to locate and extricate them and return to Nome with any supply at all. The wild, green radishes grew low in the bogs and swamps, varying in size from that of a greble ball to the larger piffle melon. Mid-August was the ripening season and, for a short week or ten days, the harvest had to be met, for little exists that is less attractive or less appetizing than an over-ripe Norton Sound green radish.

Rather like wild game, they had to be "taken," as the little devils are carnivorous, and quickly have to be covered with a tough canvas throw before small nipping jaws can come forth and inflict a painful wound.

Always I will remember Mother patiently stalking the tundra bogs, canvas throw in hand, ready to take a Norton Sound green radish at the slightest rustle of tundra grass. A good supply for winter was imperative for, as time went by, Mother's products from this worrisome perennial became widely known.

By 1943 the Norton Sound Green Radish Festival was in its eleventh gala year in Nome as an annual celebration of the harvest. The ladies of the community created, and vied with one another, for prizes made with this gastronomic delicacy. But for eleven years straight, Mother's imaginative combinations had taken the blue ribbons. Each year contests were held for the largest green radish brought in, and for the least number of bites on hands and wrists of a registered contestant. The most competitive rivalry was for the biggest prize, awarded for the most highly decorative and imaginative canvas throw. Through most of the late winter and early summer months, many of the city's ladies spent secret hours planning and executing their throw creations. Some were appliqued, others covered in fine petit-point, while a few were painted and dyed to resemble well-known Indian or Eskimo metastasis designs of the past.

That summer was an exceptional year for Norton Sound green radishes. A really bumper crop crowded the edge of every nearby swamp and muskeg pond. The festival was nearing, and everyone, it seemed, swarmed to the hinterland with canvas and bludgeon to collect a fair share for the larder. Many overstocked, and because of Mother's notoriety in preparing green radishes, bushel baskets and gunny sacks full were given to her, or simply deposited during the night on the doorstep of Sawtooth House.

Millwood was the first to comment on the glut.

"My God," he exclaimed, "What in the name of Escoffier's ghost are you going to do with all those damn green radishes? One small radish goes a bit too far all by itself, you know."

Mother remained unperturbed.

"The best laid plans of mice and men often go astray," she answered.

This reply, of course, being so astute and original, settled the matter, and the supply of Norton Sound green radishes continued to grow until most of the rear shed and a large part of the back yard were heaped to excess.

Around the table at Sawtooth House we all got a little sick of Norton Sound green radishes. Mother did her best to utilize the bountiful crop, and fairly well succeeded. Jars and tins of preserved, pickled, marinated and sweetened green radishes were stacked everywhere.

Going to bed one night near the end of August, I banged my toe on a large wooden box hidden under my bed. Curiosity prevailed, and I pulled forth an old apple crate filled to capacity with ill-appearing and dried Norton Sound green radishes.

38

It was uncanny, to turn a phrase, with what accuracy and expertise Cletus Strong could swing and empty his honey buckets. Each full bucket came around as one broad arc flying through the air, to come to an abrupt stop as the contents continued the flight into a waiting oil drum. It was a talent born of experience. The particular thud had been recognized by old Prince, and the patient horse moved the wagon on, without urging, to the next stop.

Cletus was a Texas cowpoke who had come to Alaska to escape wild horses, wild women and wild whiskey. He had found all equally stupifying in the long run and, after a night on the town, the long run is often just what he had developed.

The Hollywood cowboy image had never caught up with Cletus. Somehow he usually found himself alone in some dry hollow of the Texas plain, with a few bony and noxious steers his only companionship. In the dark, a stabbing cactus seemed always to find his elbow or buttock, and the hot shower he craved was hours away. He did not know about Alaskan horses, but he felt the women and whiskey could be no more wild in Alaska than in Texas. So, dropping saddle and reins on the spur of the moment, Cletus packed his rucksack and set out for his Promised Land.

Without too much direction or forethought Cletus had landed in Nome on a bright and sunny June day in 1936. The town was still rebuilding after the big fire of thirty-four, so he set about to help. The only job available that paid a decent wage appeared to be that of carpenter. He hired on as part of the crew rebuilding Ellerman's Hardware Store. Within ten minutes Cletus, as well as his foreman, knew he was not a carpenter. His left forefinger was red and swelling, and every board he had sawed to measurement was at least an inch short or about half an inch too long. Nothing fit. Every nail he pounded apparently had a soft lead center, as it easily bent to the side with a telltale whang that could be heard and recongnized by everyone on the job.

The desperate foreman assigned him to assist in tarring the new roof. But, after a mere thirty minutes, Cletus forgot his location and stepped backward into the hot and sticky tar to become instantly immobile. Leaving his shoes thus affixed, amid the loud blasphemy of the roofing boss, he bolted for the ladder and the relative safety of the street below. A brief conference with the foreman convinced Cletus that he was not, and never would be, a carpenter.

Somehow the only work readily available was the honey bucket wagon, languishing beside Prince's barn on upper C Street. Cletus had been raised, and had lived, rough and tough enough not to be offended by the type of work

involved. In fact he was attracted to it, for it kept him out of doors, which prospect he liked, and introduced him to a somewhat neglected Prince, with whom he established an instant and enduring friendship.

And so Cletus Strong became Nome's honey bucket man. Winter, summer, storm or shine, he and Prince made the appointed rounds, provided a necessary service to the community. Everyone liked Cletus and he liked everyone. The city had flushed a happy union.

Late one evening, after Cletus and Dottie had joined us for a wonderful dinner of regatta of sole and helmug fish with sauce guimpe de pernod, and then had left for home, someone suggested that it was strange how well Cletus had taken to his responsibilities with the honey wagon. Mother Sawtooth put aside her knitting for the moment, for already she was hard at work on next year's radish throw, and observed, "To each his own, and to own his each."

Through the years we had grown to expect wise and well thought-out responses from Mother, but this one seemed destined to be remembered. It was, as always, original and eye-catching.

A few years earlier, Cletus had "found his woman" in the person of Dottie Helman. Dottie was an active tad of a girl, barely more than five feet tall. Cletus' six-feet-four towered over her, and to see them walking together, one ever was reminded of the cartoon world's Mutt and Jeff. But it was a happy marriage that produced twin boys in its second year. Cletus was in heaven, as he wanted a son to inherit his name, until thunderstruck at the thought he must choose between his two sons to so honor one. Thus, it was decided, the first born by some forty-eight seconds became Cletus Strong, Jr., and the second was named Theodore, or Teddy, as he always was known.

Dottie was a darling and well-meaning girl, but she never could learn to spell. So her marriage license application indicated that she had been born at Oh, Clare, Wisconsin and recently had lived in Lost Angeles, California. Oh, well, mused Cletus, there were those who would agree with the latter spelling.

Dottie

39

Good news! Good news! I talked again with Mother Sawtooth about her recipes and she agreed to take the time to write them down, each with a careful explanation of method, quantity and ingredients. I was elated, overjoyed and relieved. The situation had been saved. Now, at last, page upon page was to come forth from that wonderful kitchen, rescuing forever those fantastic gourmet discoveries of this fabulous and original woman.

I could visualize the whole affair to come. First, of course, instant fame and fortune for dear Mother, a result so richly deserved, followed by a second stampede to Nome, to crowd her kitchen, to see and meet her, and to gather a stock of precious green radishes. The Norton Sound Green Radish Festival would become world renowned, organized and produced by Hollywood in Mother's honored name. Books would be published, chefs, cooks, bakers, and marlows from across the globe would come, all to seek out and know dear Mother and to learn at her elbow her celebrated secrets.

Oh, now at last, success is at hand. The world of gastronomy ever is to be rewarded!

I had purchased for Mother's use, two reams of paper of the highest quality, of course, and pens, inks, pencils and an eraser, although I knew the last named would receive little use. These accouterments I placed carefully in the middle of her kitchen table, as I knew that hint would be strong and vibrant, and hopefully, urge her to begin her writing. Then I waited, restive and uneasy.

Fall had come. The tundra bushes had turned vivid colors of red, yellow and orange. A cooler wind began to blow from the Bering Sea, carrying with it the unmistakable suggestion of winter to come. All of us at Sawtooth House, and Mother's many friends, looked forward to happy gourmet experiences around her table and to a snug and cozy winter within familiar and comfortable walls.

During the summer, Harvey had come in from the creek to visit Mother on one or two occasions but now that freezeup had come, he had returned and settled for the winter. Unusual though it was, Mother had neither sought nor found anyone to take Harvey's place, as Millwood had the season before, so the usual crisis upon Harvey's return from Dahl Creek had been averted.

As the days passed I watched with care and expectation to see if Mother had begun to write down any of her prized recipes, as she had stated she would do. For quite a while the stack of paper, inks, pens, pencils and the eraser merely sat where I had placed them. During the preparation of meals, Mother simply worked around them. Some of the bottom sheets began to show soil after a week or two, where nackel oil or begotols had been spilled, but Mother was not a messy person so such incidents were accidental and rapidly cleaned away. Several times, Eureka had asked Mother if she could not set the paper and other supplies over onto the glass-fronted kordlerack, but Mother quickly deterred her. This I took to be a good omen. She was thinking about it.

Imagine my surprise and delight when, one day, I glanced into the kitchen to see Mother, obviously concentrating, seated at her kitchen table, writing on one of the sheets of paper I had provided for her. In a frenzy of excitement I returned to my room so as not to distract her. She was doing it! She had begun. My suspicions happily were confirmed about an hour later when, tiptoeing downstairs to the kitchen, I saw that she and Eureka had gone out. There on the table lay the sheet of paper and I could not resist the temptation to peek. Oh, praise the powers on high! Without question, she had begun. In Mother's bold, round handwriting, at the top of the page I read, "Broiled grebe with acanthus conserve and willity nuts marinated in kromeskis vinegar." I could hardly contain myself. There it was, the very beginning of her noble endeavor.

"Mother, oh, Mother Sawtooth," I said aloud, "What wide horizons are opening their hearts to you!"

When Mother returned to Sawtooth House later that afternoon, I met her at the door to tell her of my delight that she at last had started to preserve her masterpieces by setting them to paper. She was not displeased by my obvious jubilation, and she smiled and said, "A watched pot never boils."

It was her usual quick and to-the-point answer and, as always, though it had certain familiar rhythm to it, it was verbose and original.

Mother appeared preoccupied. She began immediately to prepare the evening meal and did not attempt to complete the broiled grebe recipe set forth at the head of the paper.

At anchor in the roadstead off Nome was the last ship of the season, unloading its cargo before winter isolated the community. Since the city has no harbor it is necessary that all goods and passengers be transported ashore by barge. The weather was relatively calm for that time of year and the tugs, with their barges in tow, were plying the distance between ship and dock, where the long winter's supply of all necessities for the town was off-loaded.

It was Maynard's busiest time of year and he bustled about from office, to waterfront, to warehouses, to make certain all was going well. He also tended the outgoing passenger lists. It was his duty, when departure time came, to see the barge safely off to the ship with the Seattle bound passengers. When finally the ship sailed, business could settle into a slower pace for the coming months, to be aroused again in late spring when the ice had moved offshore and the first boat appeared as a dark speck on the horizon.

The sailing of the last boat was a cause for celebration in Nome. Those who had boarded the ship would be gone until spring, and those who stayed would remain part of the community through the winter. The "Last Boat Ball" was a tradition held the evening of departure. It was a gala occasion as, by attending, one could learn who had decided to remain. Word had gone through town that the *Princess of the North* was about to sail. The "Last Boat Ball" would be held that evening.

My tuxedo had been cleaned and pressed, my black tie readied. All was in order for the ball. The Nome Rhythm Players, I understood, had been practicing for weeks to provide their exceptional music. I was elated.

But it is hard for me to go on.

Mother had received a telegram that day from Kirk. I had returned to Sawtooth House in time for dinner and to dress for the Ball, when I met Mother coming out, suitcase in hand. Eureka was in tears.

"She's leaving!" Eureka cried. "Mother's going tonight on the boat!"

I could not believe what I saw or what I was hearing. Mother did not deny it. There was my ideal, my Mother Sawtooth, moving toward the door.

"But what of the recipes?" I wailed. "I've promised everyone! What of the selle of lapis, the lyonaise of microbal, the fondue of marcassin? What will I tell them?" I was near tears.

She looked at me stonily, with cold eyes, and passed through the door. I followed.

"But Mother," I pleaded. "You can't! You can't go now. What will I do?"

She turned, suitcase in hand, and tossed me the keys to Sawtooth House.

"You can't go!" I repeated. "What can I tell them?"

"Frankly, my dear, I don't give a damn!" she said. Her answer stung me. Although original, of course, it rang somewhere in my memory.

I watched her go. My beloved Mother Sawtooth. I would get her back. Somehow I would get her back. I knew I would.